by John Fante

The *Saga of Arturo Bandini*:
Wait Until Spring, Bandini (1938)
Ask the Dust (1939, 1980)
Full of Life (1952)
Dreams from Bunker Hill (1982)

Dago Red (1940)
Brotherhood of the Grape (1977)

john fante

DREAMS FROM BUNKER HILL

black sparrow press
santa barbara · 1982

LIBRARY OF CONGRESS CATALOGING IN PUBLICATION DATA

Fante, John, 1909-
    Dreams from Bunker Hill.

    I. Title.
PS3511.A594D7   813'.52   81-15533
                                            AACR2
ISBN 0-87685-529-X
ISBN 0-87685-528-1 (pbk.)
ISBN 0-87685-530-3 (signed cloth ed.)

Also for Joyce

Dreams from Bunker Hill

Chapter One

My first collision with fame was hardly memorable. I was a busboy at Marx's Deli. The year was 1934. The place was Third and Hill, Los Angeles. I was twenty-one years old, living in a world bounded on the west by Bunker Hill, on the east by Los Angeles Street, on the south by Pershing Square, and on the north by Civic Center. I was a busboy nonpareil, with great verve and style for the profession, and though I was dreadfully underpaid (one dollar a day plus meals) I attracted considerable attention as I whirled from table to table, balancing a tray on one hand, and eliciting smiles from my customers. I had something else beside a waiter's skill to offer my patrons, for I was also a writer. This phenomenon became known one day after a drunken photographer from the *Los Angeles Times* sat at the bar, snapped several pictures of me serving a customer as she looked up at me with admiring eyes. Next day there was a feature story attached to the *Times* photograph. It told of the struggle and success of young Arturo Bandini, an ambitious, hard-working kid from Colorado, who had crashed through the difficult magazine world with the sale of his first story to *The American Phoenix*, edited, of course, by the most renowned personage in American literature, none other than Heinrich Muller. Good old Muller! How I loved that man! Indeed, my first literary efforts were letters to him, asking his advice, sending him suggestions for stories I might write, and finally sending him stories too, many stories, a story a week, until even Heinrich Muller, curmudgeon of the literary world, the tiger in his lair, seemed to give up the struggle and condescended to drop me a letter with two lines in it, and then a second letter with four lines, and finally a two-page letter of twenty-four lines and then, wonder of wonders, a check for $150, payment in full for my first acceptance.

I was in rags the day that check arrived. My nondescript Colorado clothes hung from me in shreds, and my first thought was a new wardrobe. I had to be frugal but in good taste, and so I descended Bunker Hill to Second and Broadway, and the Goodwill store. I made my way to the better quality section and found an excellent blue business suit with a white pinstripe. The pants were too long and so were the sleeves, and the whole thing was ten dollars. For another dollar I had the suit altered, and while this was being taken care of, I buzzed around in the shirt department. Shirts were fifty cents apiece, of excellent quality and all manner of styles. Next I purchased a pair of shoes—fine thick-soled oxfords of pure leather, shoes that would carry me over the streets of Los Angeles for months to come. I bought other things too, several pairs of shorts and T-shirts, a dozen pairs of socks, a few neckties and finally an irresistible glorious fedora. I set it jauntily at the side of my head and walked out of the dressing room and paid my bill. Twenty bucks. It was the first time in my life that I had bought clothing for myself. As I studied my reflection in a long mirror I could not help remembering that in all my Colorado years my people had been too poor to buy me a suit of clothes, even for the graduation exercises in high school. Well, I was on my way now, nothing could stop me. Heinrich Muller, the roaring tiger of the literary world, would lead me to the top of the heap. I walked out of the Goodwill and up Third Street, a new man. My boss, Abe Marx, was standing in front of the deli as I approached.

"Good God, Bandini!" he exclaimed. "You've been to the Goodwill or something?"

"Goodwill, my ass," I snorted. "This is straight from Bullock's, you boob."

A couple of days later Abe Marx handed me a business

card. It read:

Gustave Du Mont, Ph. D.
Literary Agent
Preparation and Editing
of books, plays, scenarios, and stories
Expert editorial supervision
513 Third Street, Los Angeles
No triflers

I slipped the card into the pocket of my new suit. I took the elevator to the fifth floor. Du Mont's office was down the corridor. I entered.

The reception room lurched like an earthquake. I caught my breath and looked around. The place was full of cats. Cats on the chairs, on the valances, on the typewriter. Cats on the bookcases, in the bookcases. The stench was overpowering. The cats came to their feet and swirled around me, pressing my legs, rolling playfully over my shoes. On the floor and on the surface of the furniture a film of cat fur heaved and eddied like a pool of water. I crossed to an open window and looked down the fire escape. Cats were ascending and descending. A huge grey creature climbed toward me, the head of a salmon in his mouth. He brushed past me and leaped into the room.

By now the whir of cat fur enveloped the air. An inner office door opened. Standing there was Gustave Du Mont, a small aged man with eyes like cherries. He waved his arms and rushed among the cats shrieking,

"Out! Out! Go, everybody! Time to go home!"

The cats simply glided off at their leisure, some ending up at his feet, some playfully pawing his pants. They were his masters. Du Mont sighed, threw up his hands, and said,

"What can I do for you?"

"I'm from the deli downstairs. You left your card."

"Enter."

I stepped into his office and he closed the door. We were in a small room in the presence of three cats lolling atop a bookcase. They were elite felines, huge Persians, licking their paws with regal aplomb. I stared at them. Du Mont seemed to understand.

"My favorites," he smiled. He opened a desk drawer and drew out a fifth of Scotch.

"How about some lunch, young man?"

"No thanks, Dr. Du Mont. What did you want to see me about?"

Du Mont uncorked the bottle, took a swig from it and gasped.

"I read your story. You're a good writer. You shouldn't be slinging hash. You belong in more amenable surroundings." Du Mont took another swig. "You want a job?"

I looked at all those cats. "Maybe. What you got in mind?"

"I need an editor."

I smelled the pungency of all those cats. "I'm not sure I could take it."

"You mean the cats? I'll take care of that."

I thought a minute. "Well . . . what is it you want me to edit?"

He hit the bottle again. "Novels, short stories, whatever comes in."

I hesitated. "Can I see the stuff?"

His fist came down on a pile of manuscripts. "Help your-self."

I lifted off the top manuscript. It was a short story, written by a certain Jennifer Lovelace, entitled *Passion at Dawn*. I groaned.

Du Mont took another swig. "It's awful," he said. "They're all awful. I can't read them anymore. It's the wòrst writing I ever saw. But there's money in it if you've got the stomach. The worse they are the more you charge."

By now the whole front of my new suit was coated with cat fur. My nose itched and I felt a sneeze coming. I choked it back.

"What's the job pay?"

"Five dollars a week."

"Hell, that's only a dollar a day."

"Nothin' to it."

I snatched the bottle and took a swig. It scorched my throat. It tasted like cat piss.

"Ten dollars a week or no deal."

Du Mont shoved out his fist. "Shake," he said. "You start Monday."

Monday morning I reported for work at nine o'clock. The cats were gone. The window was closed. The reception room had been refurbished. There was a desk for me beside the window. Everything was clean and dusted. Not a single strand of cat fur clung to my finger when I rubbed it against the window sill. I sniffed the air. The urine was still potent but masked by a powerful fumigant. There was another odor too—cat repellent. I sat down at the desk and pulled out the typewriter. It was an ancient Underwood. I rolled a sheet of paper under the platen and experimented with the keyboard. The machine functioned like a rusty lawnmower. Suddenly I was dissatisfied. There was something about this job that made me apprehensive. Why should I work on somebody else's product? Why wasn't I in my room writing my own stuff? What would Heinrich Muller do in a case like this? Surely I was a fool.

The door opened and there was Du Mont. I was surprised to see him in a bowler hat, a gray vest under his frock coat, spats, and sporting a walking stick. I had never been in Paris but the sight of the natty little man made me think of the place. Was he crazy? Suddenly I thought he was.

"Good morning," he said. "How do you like your quarters?"

"What happened to the cats?"

"The fumigant," he said. "It drives them off. Don't worry. I know cats. They won't be back." He hung his hat and cane on a couple of door hooks. Then he pulled up a chair and we sat side by side at the desk. He picked up the top manuscript, *Passion at Dawn* by Jennifer Lovelace, and began to teach me the art of literary revision. He did it brutally, because in truth it was a brutal job. A black crayon in his hand, he marked and slashed and obliterated sentences, paragraphs, and whole pages. The manuscript fairly bled from the mutilation. I soon got the idea, and by the end of the day I was hacking away.

Late in the afternoon I heard a thump at my window. It was a cat, an old codger with a bruised forlorn face. He peered at me through the glass, rubbing his nose against it, then licking it expectantly. I ignored him for a few moments, and when I looked again two more cats were with him on the window sill, staring at me in orphaned alms-seeking. I couldn't take it. I went down the elevator to the deli and found some slices of pastrami in the garbage can. I wrapped them in a napkin and brought them back to the cats. When I opened the window they burst into the room and ate ravenously from my hand.

I heard Du Mont laughing. He was in the doorway of his office, one of his three Persians in his arms.

"I knew you were a cat man," he said. "I could tell from your eyes."

Chapter Two

It took me three days to revise Jennifer Lovelace's story. Her version had been thirty pages long. Mine reduced the manuscript down to half of that. It really wasn't a bad story; it was simply bad construction and phrasing, the story of six school teachers riding in a covered wagon across the plains, having skirmishes with Indians and outlaws, and finally arriving in Stockton. I was pleased with what I had done and took the manuscript to Du Mont. He hefted it and frowned.

"Couldn't you add another ten pages?" he asked.

"It's long enough," I insisted. "I won't add another line. I think Jennifer Lovelace is going to like it."

He reached for the telephone. "I'll tell her the script is ready."

I was feeding the cats next afternoon when Jennifer arrived. Her beauty was staggering. She was in a white linen suit with sheer black stockings and black pumps, a black purse hanging from her arm. Her hair was a froth of shimmering black, her face exquisite, illumined by black eyes. There was so much to see as I looked at her, and my eyes fell upon the contour of her body, the sensuality of her waist and hips, tantalizing, challenging, unbelievable. I had looked at thousands of beautiful women since arriving in Los Angeles but Jennifer Lovelace's beauty had me by the throat.

"Hi," I said, and stumbled to my feet.

"Good afternoon," she smiled. "I'm Jennifer Lovelace. Is Dr. Du Mont here?"

"I'll see. Please sit down."

She floated down into a chair like a lovely satin pillow and I watched the mechanics of her knees, her thighs, her hips. She folded her exquisite hands in her lap and I felt a gloat of pleasure. I tapped Du Mont's door and he called to me to enter. I went in, carefully closed the door and whispered, "She's here!"

"Shh!" Du Mont said, pressing his lips. "Let her wait awhile. She's rich."

"She *looks* rich."

Du Mont pulled a gold watch from his vest pocket and stared at it for what seemed a long time. Then he snapped, "Now! Show her in!"

I opened the door and found her sitting there in patient aplomb, like a queen.

"Please come in," I said.

"Thank you," she said, rising. As she stepped toward Du Mont's office I saw the back of her suit covered with cat fur.

"Wait!" I said. She paused and looked at me puzzled. Here was my chance. I dropped to my knees behind her and began brushing away the cat fur from her glorious buttocks, feeling the taut muscled thighs, the roundness of her effulgent rear. She whirled away from me.

"What are you doing?" she demanded. "What on earth?"

"The cats," I said, holding out my two hands covered with cat fur.

She twisted her torso to look at the clinging fur, and began to brush it away with one hand. I crawled to her assistance and she pushed me away.

"Please!" she implored. "Leave me alone." By now Du Mont was at her side, gallant, collected.

"Come, my dear," he soothed, leading her through the door, then closing it behind her. I knelt on the floor, confused and embarrassed, as the cats swirled around me, whining to be fed.

There was a silence in Du Mont's office. On my knees I peered through the keyhole at Jennifer seated across the desk from Du Mont. Her face was a furious frown as she read the revised version of her story.

"My manuscript!" she gasped. "What happened to it?" She groped through her purse. "Give me a cigarette, please."

Du Mont proffered one.

"What have you done to my story, Dr. Du Mont? You've destroyed it—my beautiful story! How could you do this to me?"

Du Mont lifted his palms placatingly. "I did nothing, my dear," he lied. "I had no idea that he was doing it."

Jennifer Lovelace stiffened. "He? Who's he?"

Du Mont didn't say a word. He merely nodded guiltily at the reception room door. As Jennifer Lovelace leaped to her feet I took off—into the hall, down the stairs, through the deli, and out the back way to the alley. There I found a packing box and sat upon it and smoked a cigarette, my hands trembling. About me I noticed the cats, the same old gang who visited my office. They looked at me curiously, wondering what I was doing in their territory.

I looked up at the window of my office. I couldn't go back there. I wouldn't. I felt betrayed. Du Mont had tricked me. The savage editing of Jennifer's script filled me with shame now. If someone had hacked up my work like that I would have punched him. I wondered what Heinrich Muller would say about my integrity. Integrity! I laughed. Integrity—balls. I was a nothing, a zero. To hell with it. I decided to go shopping for a pair of pants. I still had over a hundred dollars. I would splurge and forget my troubles in profligate spending. What was money anyway?

At the Goodwill I selected and tried on three pairs of pants. Somehow they did very little for me. I looked at myself in the long, mirror, and there I was—the cipher, the zero. Shameful in the presence of Heinrich Muller, the lion of literature.

Walking across Third and Hill to Angel's Flight, I climbed aboard the trolley and sat down. The only other passenger was a girl across the aisle reading a book. She was in a plain dress and without stockings. She was rather attractive but not my style. As the trolley lurched into motion she moved to another seat. No ass at all, I thought. An ass, yes, but without the splendor of Jennifer Lovelace's. Without nobility, without the grandeur of a thing of beauty. Just an ass, a plain common ass. It was not my day.

I got off the cablecar at the top of Angel's Flight and started down Third Street toward my hotel. Then I decided on a cup of coffee and a cigarette in the small Japanese restaurant a few doors ahead. The coffee erased my gloom and I walked on to my hotel. The landlady sat behind the desk in the lobby. The first thing I noticed was a copy of *The American Phoenix.* It was exactly where I had placed it three weeks ago. Annoyed, I walked boldly to the desk and picked it up.

"You haven't read it, have you?"

She smiled, hostile. "No, I haven't."

"Why not?" I said.

"It bored me. I read the first paragraph and that was enough for me."

I put the magazine under my arm.

"I'm moving out," I said. "Real soon."

"Suit yourself."

I walked away and down the hall. As I turned the key in my door I heard the click of a lock across the hall. The door opened and the girl from the trolley stepped out. She still carried the book. It was Zola's *Nana.* She smiled in greeting.

"Hi!" I said. "I didn't know you lived here."

"I just moved in."

"You work around here?"

"I suppose you'd call it that." She made a sensual glance. "Would you like to see me?"

"When?"

"How about right now?"

I didn't want her. Nothing of her lured me, but I had to be manly. These situations could only be resolved in one way.

"Sure," I said.

She turned on the tiny flame of sensuality in her eyes and

pushed open her door.

"What are we waiting for?" she said.

I hesitated. Lord help me, I thought, as I crossed the hall and entered her room.

She followed me inside and closed the door.

"What's your name, honey?"

"Arturo," I said. "Arturo Bandini."

She held out her hands and removed my coat.

"How much?" I asked.

"A fin."

She guided me around to face her and began unbuttoning my shirt. Hanging it over a chair she crossed to the bathroom.

"See you in a minute."

She entered the bathroom and closed the door. I sat on the bed and pulled off my clothes. I was naked when she emerged. I tried to hide my disappointment. She was clean and bathed but somehow impure. Her bottom hung there like an orphan child. We would never make it together. My presence there was insanity. She grasped my rod and led me to the bathroom. She washed and soaped my loins and her fingers kneaded my joint determinedly, but there was no response. I could only think of Jennifer Lovelace and the gallantry of her flanks. Then she towelled me off and we went back to the bedroom and lay on the bed. She spread herself out naked and I lay beside her.

"Go ahead," she said. I traced one finger through her pubic hair.

"Do you mind if I read?" she said. "Hand me my book."

I gave her the book and she opened it to her place and began to read. I lay there and wondered. Good God, what if my mother were to walk in? Or my father? Or Heinrich Muller? Where would it all end? She nodded toward a bowl of apples at the bedside.

"Want an apple?" she asked.

"No thanks."

"Give me one please."

I handed her an apple. And so she read and ate.

"Come on, honey," she coaxed. "Enjoy yourself."

I swung my legs out of bed and stood up.

"What's the matter?" she asked, her voice hostile.

"Don't worry. I'll pay you off."

"Would you like me to suck you?"

"No," I said.

She slammed the book shut.

"Do you know what's the matter with you, sonny? You're queer. That's what's the matter with you. You're a fag. I know your kind."

She grabbed my coat, pants, underwear, shoes and socks, raced to the door and threw it all in the hall. I stepped out and began gathering my things.

"I owe you five bucks," I said.

"No, you don't. You don't owe me a thing."

I groped through my coat pocket for the door key. Down the hall, watching me with her arms folded, was Mrs. Brownell, the landlady. I turned the key and jumped into my room.

I felt relieved, saved, rescued. I went to the window to look at all of the great city spread below me. It was like a view of the whole world. Far to the southwest the sun struck the ocean in bars of heavenly light. A message from God. A sign. The Infant Jesus in the manger, the light from the Star of Bethlehem. I fell on my knees.

"Oh blessed Infant Jesus," I prayed. "Thank you for saving me this day. Bless you for the surge of God's goodness that moved me from that room of sin. I swear it now—I will never sin again. For the rest of my life I will remember your glorious intercession. Thank you, little Son of God. I am your devoted servant forever henceforth."

I made the sign of the cross and got to my feet. How good I felt. How recharged with the feelings of my early boyhood. I had to get in touch with Jennifer Lovelace. I dressed and went out to the lobby. At the pay station I dialed Du Mont's number.

"What happened to you?" he asked.

"I'm at my hotel. What's Jennifer Lovelace's phone

number?"

He gave it to me and I wrote it down.

I went back to my room and sat at the typewriter. I typed for fifteen minutes—two pages of heartbreak. I folded the paper and walked out of the hotel to the pay station across the street and telephoned Jennifer. Unfolding my notes, I heard the telephone ringing.

"Hello." It was she.

"Jennifer, this is Arturo Bandini."

There was a silence. The sweat popped from my skin. My voice quivered.

"Jennifer, I want you to forgive me. I don't know why I destroyed your beautiful manuscript. It was simply a matter of inexperience. I'm a good writer, Jennifer. I can prove that. I'll bring you some of my work. You'll see what a superb writer I am. I didn't mean to ruin your manuscript. I'm not a critic, Jennifer. I only followed Du Mont's instruction. I made a terrible mistake. Won't you let me see you and explain? I'd like to tell you what a wonderful talent I am. Please, Jennifer. Give me the chance to explain. . . ."

There was more to say, but she cut in.

"How about Sunday?"

"Any day, any time. You name it."

She gave me her address in Santa Monica and I wrote it down.

"Thank you, Jennifer. You won't regret this."

She hung up.

Chapter Three

The sun hit my face like big golden eye, wakening me. It was Sunday morning and it promised a bright and glorious day. I shot out of bed, opened the window wide and called out to the world, hello everybody! Good luck to all! A good day, a fresh day. I remembered my father in Colorado at the kitchen sink on a bright spring morning, singing with happiness as he shaved. *O Sole Mio.* I stood before my bathroom mirror and sang it too. Oh God, how good I felt! How was it possible? For breakfast I peeled and ate two oranges.

In my fine Goodwill pinstripe suit and my rakish fedora, I tucked a copy of *The American Phoenix* under my arm and strode out to conquer a woman. Down Olive Street I marched on the clear Sunday morning. The city seemed deserted, the street was quiet. I paused and listened. I heard something. It was the sound of happiness. It was my own heart beating softly, rhythmically. A clock, that's what I was, a little happiness machine. I crossed Fifth Street to the Biltmore Hotel. Well-dressed folk moved in and out through the revolving doors. They were people like myself, neatly attired, the better class. At the main entrance stood a uniformed doorman. He looked ten feet tall as he saluted me. I returned the salute.

"Do you have the time, sir?" I asked.

"Yes, sir." He glanced at his wristwatch. "It's eleven o'clock, sir."

"Thank you, sir."

I walked to the curbing and looked at a long line of taxi cabs, a waiting driver in each. Suddenly an idea exploded in my head. I would take a taxi to Jennifer's. All my life I had wanted to take a taxi, but for a number of reasons, all financial, I had never done so. Now I could do it. I could arrive in style. I could sweep up to her house, wait for the driver to open the door, then leap out like a prince. The doorman came to my side.

"Taxi, sir?"

"Yes, sir." He opened the door of the nearest taxi and I got inside. The driver swung around and looked at me.

"Where to, sir?"

"1724 Eighteenth Street, Santa Monica."

"Pretty long fare," he said.

"It's of no consequence," I answered. "No consequence at all."

The cab drew away from the curb, turned right on Seventh Street, then right on Hope Street to Wilshire Boulevard. I watched the street and the shops and felt a lump in my throat. What a wonderful city! Look at all those beautiful people walking in their fine garments as they came from churches and window shopped along the bright boulevard. No doubt about it, this was my day, my city.

The cab driver was right. It was a long fare—seven dollars and twenty cents worth. He punched the meter and I studied the final figure. I stepped out of the cab and handed the driver a ten-dollar bill. He dug out the exact change, which I counted. Then it occurred to me that tipping was also the custom. He was watching me. I handed him a dime.

His lip curled. "Gee, thanks."

I turned away and looked at Jennifer's house. It was out of Mother Goose, a yellow and white Victorian fantasy with cupolas at both corners of the second story. The cupolas were adorned with wood panels of carved spools and intricate patterns of scrolls and twirling figures. It was a wedding cake, complete in every detail except the bride and groom. It sat there proudly in an enclosure of huge fir trees, strangely out of place, belonging instead to the Land of Oz. Jennifer's house! I saw the big comfortable chairs on the veranda and smiled at the thought that her marvellous bottom had graced them all.

She came to the door as I mounted the porch stairs.

"Hello!" she smiled. "I'm glad you came. Please come in."

She pushed open the screen door and I walked inside. The room was dazzling. A grand piano, luxurious chairs, gigantic Boston ferns, Tiffany lamps, and a large painting in oils above the fireplace—of a child with long curls. She permitted me enough time to study the portrait as she explained that it was a painting of herself.

"Do sit down," she said. "Mother and Dad are at mass. They should be back soon."

"Did you go to mass this morning?" I asked.

"Oh, yes. Are you a Catholic?"

"What else?" I smiled. "The church has been part of my family for generations."

"Then you went to mass this morning?"

"Naturally. Missing mass is a mortal sin. Surely you know that."

She smiled. "Of course."

I sat down. "As a matter of fact I had something of a theological dispute with my confessor this morning."

She smoothed out the seat of her yellow sun suit as she sat down. Her bottom filled the chair like a lovely egg in a nest.

"Where's your parish?" she asked.

I knew that somewhere in Los Angeles there had to be a St. Mary's Church, and I answered, "Saint Mary of Guadalupe."

"Isn't it gorgeous?" she exclaimed. "I love that church."

"I often pray there."

"You were saying something about a dispute with your confessor. What did you mean?"

"I'll tell you, but only in strictest confidence. The sacred seal of the confessional."

She gasped and her hand touched her bosom. "Should you?" she asked.

"I must," I said. I wrung my hands in my lap for a moment or two and then I continued.

"You remember the debauchery of your manuscript? Have you forgotten how I destroyed it in wanton disregard for your feelings? Have you forgotten your anger at the outrage?"

She nodded solemnly.

"When I entered the confessional and faced the priest my one question was—had I committed a mortal sin in ruining your work? Was it an extreme offense against the law of God? Would he forgive me for it? The priest looked at me through the screen and thought a moment, and then he said, 'The desecration of any artistic achievement is one of the great sins against the law of God.'"

She seemed terribly impressed and stood up.

"Would you like a coke, Mr. Bandini?"

"Yes, thank you."

She walked quickly toward the kitchen, her glorious ass following her in ritualistic cadence.

I went after her and she took a couple of cokes from the refrigerator and handed one to me. We opened the bottles and drank. There was a covered picnic basket on the table. I lifted the lid and peeked inside.

"That's for us," she said.

"We're going someplace?"

"The beach."

"The ocean?"

"Naturally."

"Can we swim?"

"That's what it's for."

"I don't have any swimming trunks."

"You can borrow a pair of my brother's."

We finished our cokes.

"Let's go," she said.

Carrying the picnic basket, I followed her down the back stairs to the garage where a two-door Chevy was parked. I put the basket in the back seat and slid in beside her. She started the engine and drove down the alley to the cross street and turned into traffic.

A mile north of the Santa Monica pier on the Pacific Coast Highway was a cluster of beach bungalows, weather beaten and very old. We drew to the curb and got out. A wooden path led us through a high fence to one of a dozen cottages built on the sand. She turned a key in the door of the first cottage and we went inside. The bungalow belonged to her family. It was not pretentious—a stove, a refrigerator, table and chairs. Off the kitchen were two bedrooms. She went into one and emerged in a black bathing suit, tossing me a pair of trunks. While I undressed she went outside and ran toward the surf. I stripped off my clothes and frowned at my lily-white body. It reminded me of a pink pig, and I dreaded the shock in her face when I made my appearance. But she wasn't shocked at all as she lay on the warm sand and read *The American Phoenix* through dark horn-rimmed glasses.

The ocean was staggering. I forgot my pale, sunless body and stared in wonder. The beach was almost deserted. A group of children came trotting past, stopping to stare at me; then giggling, they trotted on. Carefully I permitted the small waves to cover my toes as I splashed along in pleasure. Gradually I moved into deeper water and began to swim, invigorated by the cool tangy surf. Colorado seemed an eternity away. I told myself that at this moment my mother had arrived home from mass and was preparing lunch. She was probably thinking of me even as I thought of her.

I kept glancing at Jennifer. She was absorbed in the magazine and paid no attention to me. I stood before her and caught her attention.

"Watch!"

I did a handspring, then another, and a third. She smiled vaguely and turned back to the magazine. I had other tricks, for I had been a member of the tumbling team at Colorado University.

"Watch this one!"

I did a number of cartwheels. She looked up and gave me a distracted smile.

"Watch this!"

I got up on my hands and walked out into the water until my hands and shoulders were submerged. Then I tumbled off my balance. I looked toward the beach. Jennifer was gone. I saw her wade through the sand and enter the cottage. I went after her.

She was taking things from the picnic basket—lettuce, onions, tomatoes—washing them in the sink, then cutting them up in a wooden bowl. She had put on a cocktail apron over her sleek black bathing suit. It made me gape. Her figure was voluptuous, tantalizing, irresistible. I lit a cigarette and my hand shook, and I thought the moment has come. It's now or never. Don't be a dummy. Act. This time will never come again. Be brave. You've got nothing to lose. Everything to gain. I stood up and flung myself at her, falling to my knees and throwing my arms around her waist.

"I love you," I said. "I want you."

She twisted her superb hips to escape my grip. I clung like a tiger. She lifted the salad bowl and brought it down on my head. I felt the inundation of mayonnaise, olive oil and vegetables as I sprawled on the floor, dragging her down upon me.

"You fool!" she screamed. "Let me go! You crazy fool!"

We were caught up in some sort of inexplicable violence, wrestling with one another, sliding across the floor, fighting a meaningless combat. She screamed when I bit her ass. She got to her hands and knees and crawled out of my grasp and into the bedroom, kicking the door closed.

I sat panting in the quagmire of salad dressing. What had I done? On the messy floor was my copy of *The American Phoenix*, smeared with oil and mayonnaise. What now, I asked. Go, I said. Take flight. Get out of here. I crawled into a chair and saw scratch marks on my chest and legs. The end of the world. The end of me. The end of my love. The bedroom door opened and she stepped out. She was towelling off her body, smearing away the salad dressing. She didn't say a word.

"I'm sorry," I said.

"You sonofabitch!" she said. She picked up her keys from the table and went to the door. "And another thing," she snapped, "there's no such church as St. Mary's of Guadalupe!"

She went out. I followed her through the front gate to the highway. She entered her car and drove away.

I wanted to cry, but my stupidity overwhelmed me. I went back to the bungalow, took off the bathing trunks and got under a cold shower. I towelled myself off, dressed, closed the cottage doors, and stepped out beside the highway. Across the street bathers were climbing down the steep path from the top of the palisades. I crossed the highway and started up the path. It took me to Ocean Avenue and a street car depot. I took the next car and rode back to my hotel.

As I turned the key in my door I heard a radio playing across the hall. The song was *Begin the Beguine.* I entered my room, took off my clothes, and put on a bathrobe. It was almost dark now, dark, lonely and erotic. I left my room, crossed the hall, and knocked on her door. The radio went off and she called,

"Come in."

I opened the door.

She was stretched out on the bed dressed in a pink slip, still reading *Nana.* She frowned.

"What do *you* want?"

"Let's fuck," I said.

Chapter Four

The days stumbled past. August came, hot and sticky. One evening it rained. People streamed out of the hotel and stood in the street catching the rain in their hands. A sweet smell came over Bunker Hill. The rain splashed our faces. Then it was gone. I worked hard, pecking away on a short story. I took the work with me to Du Mont's office. Several times during the day he drifted over and studied what I was writing. Suddenly he tore the page from my typewriter.

"You're fired," he said. He was trembling. "Take your story and get out."

I left. I went to a movie. I loafed down Main Street to the Follies, the marquee lit with the name of Ginger Britton. She was in the midst of her strip, swinging from the drapes, her ass a perfect Rubens. I found a seat in the first row and watched her ravenously. She was magnificent, with the ass of a young colt, stomping the stage in high heels, turning her back on the audience, bending down to look at us between her legs. An absolutely world-champion ass, incomparable, her skin glowing like the meat of a honeydew melon. Her long red hair hung to her hips, her Valkyrie breasts flying about in wild circles. The audience cheered and whistled. They angered me. Why were they so fucking vulgar? They were watching a work of art with the same acclaim as a boxing match. It was sacrilegious. As she left the stage the applause was raucous, impossible. I couldn't bear it, and stomped out of the theater. In a rage I returned to my hotel. I sat at the typewriter and wrote a letter to Ginger Britton:

Dear Ginger Britton:
I love you. I saw you today and I love you madly. I reverence you. I long to know you, to talk to you, to hold your hand, to take you in my arms and smother you with kisses. The sight of you dancing was like a flame through my body. What I would give to take you to dinner in some quiet supper club, your red hair in my face, your lips wet with wine, kissing mine! Be kind to me, dear lady of the Follies, and invite me to visit you some evening after the show. I tremble with love.

Arturo Bandini

I signed the letter, put it in an envelope and took it to the lobby. Mrs. Brownell was behind the desk. I asked her for a stamp. Then I smelled an intoxicating odor wafted from the door of her living quarters behind the desk.

"What's that?" I asked, sniffing.

"Mince pie," she said. "I just took it out of the oven."

"Smells wonderful."

"Would you like a piece?"

It was the first friendly remark I ever heard from her. I looked at her clear blue eyes and wondered at the change. She was actually hospitable and not the bitch I had gotten used to.

"Thank you, Mrs. Brownell. I'd love a piece."

She invited me into her room. I stood there looking around. It was a housekeeping room—a stove, a refrigerator, a breakfast table, a couple of chairs, and a studio couch.

"Sit down, Mr. Bandini."

I sat at the table and watched her cut a wedge from a large mince pie. She wasn't young. Maybe fifty-five. If you looked closely you saw that her figure was trim and well formed. There was even a hint of a nice ass. She placed the wedge of pie in a deep plate and poured brandy over it.

"It's funny," she said. "All this hot day I've been thinking of mince pie. Now I know why." She smiled, her perfect dentures showing, and put the pie before me. She handed me a spoon, and I tasted the pie. I must have eaten very quickly, for she soon served me a second piece. It was very powerful pie, but I loved it, and sipped the brandy like soup, and felt great heat in my stomach. Then everything was vague and I was drunk. I heard Mrs. Brownell talking of Kansas and Thanksgiving dinner on a farm outside of Topeka, an account of her brothers and sisters and how her father ran away with a woman from Wichita.

I woke up in bed. Not my bed, but Mrs. Brownell's. I lay on my back next to the wall. The person asleep at my side was Mrs. Brownell. She was in a white nightgown and nightcap. She lay facing me, her two hands clutching my arm as she snored musically. The bedside clock showed three A.M. I closed my eyes and went back to sleep.

We were good for each other, Helen Brownell and I. Every night I found the passage to her room an easy journey. She sometimes smiled as I sat down and removed my shoes. Other times she paid no attention, as if expecting me. I was her little champion, she said, for I was a small man, no larger than her husband, an accountant who had died five years before. When it was time to close up shop she disappeared into the bathroom to undress, then emerging in her muslin nightie and nightcap. She snapped off the bathroom light and slipped into bed beside me. We shared the darkness together, sometimes, that is. Sometimes I groped a little and she responded. Mostly she was like a relative in the night, a maiden aunt, my Aunt Cornelia who lived with us when I was a boy and who hated children. In the morning I awoke to the hiss of bacon, and saw her over the stove, cooking my breakfast.

"Good morning," I'd say, and she'd answer,

"Time for breakfast, little champ."

Sometimes she bent over and kissed me on the forehead. She must have known that I was broke for every day or two I found a couple of dollars in my pocket. I tried to do the dishes, but she wouldn't have it. Well fed and rested I went down to my room and faced the black monster typewriter glaring at me with gaping white teeth. Sometimes I wrote ten pages. I didn't like that, for I knew that whenever I was prolific I also stank. I stank most of the time. I had to be patient. I knew it would come. Patience! It was the least of my virtues.

One day there was a surprise in my mail. The letter sparkled in my hand. I recognized it instantly. It was a letter from Ginger Britton, scented with the fragrance of gardenias. I took it to my room and sat on the bed and opened it, a letter in a stately hand of elegant penmanship. Ginger Britton thanked me for my letter. She appreciated all that I had written and she was delighted. Unfortunately she could not meet me for a supper date because she was certain her husband would never permit it, but she urged me to come often to the Follies to watch her perform. She loved my letter. She was deeply moved by it. She would treasure it always.

I unfolded the letter and pressed it to my face, breathing the fragrance of her gardenias. I pressed my lips into it and gurgled gratefully. Da, da, da I murmured. Oh Ginger Britton, how I love you! Da da da.

I was in the first row of the Follies Theater when the curtain rose for the burlesque show. She entered the stage with the full cast and I sank gratefully into my seat. I had come with plans: to whisper to her, to wave, to toss her a kiss, but as I looked around, every face was the face of her husband, and I lost courage. Then I looked up at her face. She was smiling down at me. She recognized me. I *knew* that she recognized me, and there was an intimacy about her smile that thrilled me, and I waved two or three fingers in a cowardly acknowledgment. Then she entered her specialty routine, twirling midstage, then bending backward to look at the audience between her legs, and from that position she turned her face to me and smiled emphatically. I looked about nervously. The customers ignored me except a man two aisles back, a black man, rugged, tough, unsmiling, staring straight at me. I sensed trouble, got up and walked out. The black man was either her husband or another fan who had written her.

Chapter Five

On the way back to Bunker Hill I went through Pershing Square. It was a warm night and the park was brilliant beneath the street lamps. People sat on park benches enjoying the cool tranquillity after a hot day. In the center of the square was a park bench occupied by chess players. There were four players on either side of the long table, each with a chessboard in front of him. They were playing rapid transit chess—eight players matching their skills against one man, an old man, a raucous, insolent, brilliant man in shirt sleeves, dancing about as he moved from player to player, making a chess move, delivering an insult, then moving on to the next player. In a matter of minutes he had checkmated all eight of his opponents and snatched up a bet of twenty-five cents for his victory. As the disgruntled players moved away, the old man, whose name was Mose Moss, shouted out,

"Who's next? Who thinks he's a great chess player? I'll beat any man here, any two men, any ten men." He whirled and looked at me.

"What are you standing there for?" he shouted. "Who the hell do you think you are? You got two bits? Sit down, and put it up, you smart-ass kid. I'll beat your britches off!"

I turned away.

"That's it!" he sneered. "You fucking coward! I knew you was yellow the minute I laid eyes on you!"

By now another group of chess players had taken seats around the long table. There were seven of them. I had not played chess in two years, but I had been a good chess player at Colorado, and had even won a tournament at the chess club. I knew I could hold my own against this garrulous, insulting old bastard, but I didn't know if I could win against his scatological attack. He slapped me on the back.

"Sit down, sonny. Learn something about chess."

That did it. I dug a quarter from my pocket, slapped it on the table, and sat down.

He beat me and the others in ten moves. We, the victims, rose from the table as he gathered up the quarters and jingled them in his pocket.

"Is it over?" he asked. "Have I won again?"

I dug out another quarter, but the other players had had enough. Mose Moss sat across from me and we began to play. He lit a cigarette.

"Who taught you this game, kid? Your mother?"

"Your move," I said. "You sonofabitch!"

"Now you're sounding like real chess player," he said, moving a pawn. He beat me in twelve moves. I plumped down another quarter. He beat me again quickly, decisively. There was no way I could defeat this old man. Then he began to toy with me. It was cruel. It was brutal. It was sadistic. He offered to engage me without his queen, and I lost. Next he removed his queen, his two bishops, and his two knights, and I lost again. Finally he stripped his forces down to just pawns. By now a crowd three deep was gathered about us, howling with laughter as his pawns mowed my pieces down and he worked another checkmate. I had one quarter left. I placed it on the table. Mose Moss rubbed his hands together and smiled with benign triumph.

"Tell you what I'm going to do now, kid. I'm going to let you win. You're going to checkmate me."

The audience applauded, moved closer. Forty people crowded about. He needed about twenty moves to finish me off, maneuvering his pieces in such a way that I could not avoid checkmating him. I was tired, frustrated, and sick of soul. My stomach ached, my eyes burned.

"I'm through, Mose," I said. "That was my last quarter."

"Your credit is good," he said. "You look like an honest

kid. You're a goddamn fool, but you look honest."

Numbly I began to play, too confused to walk away, too ashamed to get to my feet and move off. Suddenly there was a commotion. The bystanders fled. The police were on the scene. They grabbed a couple of people and Mose and I were hustled off to the paddy wagon. We were taken to the city jail, six of us, and lined up at the sergeant's desk, each accused of loitering. After the booking, we were taken to the drunk tank. I followed Mose around, for he seemed to know the routine. We sat on a bench and I asked Mose what happened next.

"Ten dollars or five days," he said. "Fuck 'em. Let's play chess." To my horror he pulled a miniature chess game from his back pocket, and we put the chess men into place and began to play. He was indefatigable. My eyes would not open. I slept with my chin on my chest. He shook me awake and I moved a player. We were playing for astronomical sums now. I owed him fifteen thousand dollars. We doubled it. I lost again, and as Mose tried to awaken me, I slipped off the bench and fell asleep on the floor. I heard his last words:

"You bastard, you owe me thirty thousand dollars."

"Put it on my bill," I said.

I slept. Vaguely I heard the night sounds around me—the snores, the farts, the moans, the puking, the mumbling in sleep. It was cold in the big cell. The gray dawn crept through the window. Daylight gradually came. At six o'clock the jailer rattled the cell bars with a riot stick.

"Everybody get ready for Sunrise Court," he shouted. "You have five minutes to make a phone call."

I followed Mose down the hall to a waiting room with telephones on the wall. They were pay phones. I searched my pockets for a dime. I had nothing. Mose was in front of me, talking to someone by phone. As he hung up I crowded him.

"Loan me a dime," I said.

He frowned. "Jesus, kid," he said. "You already owe me

thirty grand."

"I'll pay you back, Mose," I implored. "Every cent. Believe me."

He dug into his pocket and pulled out a handful of silver coins. "Take one."

I selected a dime and stepped up to the telephone. I dialled my hotel. Mrs. Brownell answered.

"I'm in Sunrise Court," I told her. "Can you bail me out? It's ten dollars."

There was a silence. "Are you in trouble?"

"No, but I'm broke."

"I'll be right there." She hung up.

She was in the courtroom when the prisoners were brought in. My name was called and I approached the bench. The judge never saw me, never even looked at me.

"You are charged with loitering. Ten dollars or five days. How do you plead?"

"Guilty," I said.

"Pay the bailiff," he said. "Next."

As I moved to the bailiff's desk Mrs. Brownell arose and came to my side. She opened her purse and gave the bailiff a ten-dollar bill. I bent over the desk and signed a bail receipt. Mrs. Brownell sped down the hall, moving fast. I ran to catch her.

"Thanks," I said. She raced ahead, out the front door, down the steps to the street, where her car was parked. I got in beside her, and the car lurched as she threw it into gear.

"I appreciate what you did," I said. She flung me a bitter glance.

"Jailbird!" she said. We did not speak as she drove up Temple Street and turned onto Bunker Hill. She parked the car in the empty lot next to the hotel.

"I didn't commit a crime," I explained. "I was booked for playing chess, that's all."

She looked sullen. "And now you have a prison record."

"Oh shit," I said.

We got out and crossed to the hotel. We went through the office into her living quarters. She stepped into the bathroom and turned on the hot water. Clouds of steam rose and drifted into the living room.

"You're going to take a bath," she said. "You're going to cleanse yourself of all that jailhouse scruff and dirt and filth, the lice and fleas and bedbugs."

I dropped my clothes around my feet and she gathered them like dead animals and tossed them into the laundry hamper. The water was warm and soapy, and I sank to my neck and let the goodness of heat sink in. Mrs. Brownell bent over me with a washcloth and a lump of fels naphtha soap. She lathered the washcloth and began to scrub me. The washcloth ground into my ears until I screamed.

"Dirt," she said. "Look at the dirt! Aren't you ashamed?"

She plunged the washcloth into my crotch and I screamed again.

"Get out," I said. "Leave me alone."

She flung the washcloth into my face. "Jailbird!" she said. "Convict!"

She turned and left me alone. I dried myself off, got into my shorts and walked into the kitchen. She was at the stove, cooking my breakfast, her back to me. Skilled ass man that I was, I quickly detected the contraction of her buttocks—a sure sign of rage in a woman. Experience had taught me great caution in the face of such dramatic change in the derrière and I was quiet as I sat down. It was like being in the presence of a coiled snake. She brought ham and eggs to the table and slammed the dish in front of me. The telephone rang. I heard her answer it.

"For you," she said.

I picked up the phone. The caller was Harry Schindler, the movie director. He was an old friend of H. L. Muller. He had obtained my address from Muller, and was anxious to talk to me.

"What about?"

"Have you ever written for pictures?"

"No."

"That's fine," Schindler said. "Would you like a job?"

"Doing what?"

"Writing a screenplay."

"I don't know how."

"Nothing to it," Schindler said. "I'll show you. Meet me at Columbia Pictures tomorrow morning at ten o'clock."

I went back to Mrs. Brownell's living room and sat down. She had obviously overheard the telephone conversation.

"I may have a job in the movies."

"At least you'll be clean," she said. I noticed her derrière. It was still contracted. I ate quickly and went back to my room.

Chapter Six

Next morning Mrs. Brownell gave me directions and I took the Sunset bus to Gower Avenue. The studio was down the street half a block. I took the elevator to the fourth floor and found Schindler's office. His secretary sat at her desk reading a novel. She was blonde, with her hair severely coiffured, drawn back to a knot at the nape of her neck. She had golden eyebrows and her eyes were pure topaz, hostile, not friendly.

"Yes?" she said.

I told her my name. She rose and moved to Schindler's office door. Her dress was green velvet. Instantly I was aware of her sensational ass, a Hollywood perfecto. She moved like a snake, a large snake, a lustful boa constrictor. I was very pleased. She knocked on Schindler's door and opened it.

"Mr. Bandini," she announced.

Schindler rose from his desk and we shook hands.

"Sit down," he said. "Make yourself at home."

He was a short, bullet-shaped man with a crew cut, an unlit cigar in his mouth.

"I've read all of your published stories," he said. "You've got lots of style, kid. You're just what I need. H. L. Muller strikes again!" he laughed. "We're old friends, H. L. Muller and I. We worked on the *Baltimore Sun* together. I've known him for twenty years."

"I told you I've never written for pictures. Don't expect too much."

"Leave that to me," Schindler said.

"Just what did you have in mind?"

"Nothing, for the time being. First, get used to the place. Get acclimated. Get oriented. Read some of my screenplays, look at some of my films. Meet the other writers on this floor—Benchley, Ben Hecht, Dalton Trumbo, Nat West. You're in good company, kid."

"Does Sinclair Lewis work here?" I asked.

"I wish he did. Why? Do you know Lewis?"

"He's my favorite American writer."

"And a good friend of H. L. Muller," Schindler smiled. He pushed a buzzer and the secretary came in.

"Set Mr. Bandini up in the other office," Schindler told her. "Arrange for him to look at some of my films, and see that he gets some of my screenplays."

We shook hands.

"Good luck, Bandini. We're going to do great things together."

"I hope so."

I turned to leave.

"By the way," he said, "do you two know one another?"

I said no, and the girl said nothing.

"Arturo," Schindler said, "meet your secretary, Thelma Farber."

I smiled at her. "Hi."

I wasn't sure, but I thought I saw her lip curl. She turned and walked out, and I followed the undulations of the boa constrictor in the green velvet dress. We crossed the reception room to an adjoining office. I looked around. A desk, a couple of chairs, a couch, a typewriter, some empty bookshelves.

"Fine," I said. "What do I do now?"

"Suit yourself," she said, and promptly walked out and closed the door. I wondered about her, puzzled. Then I opened the door. She was at her desk reading her novel.

"Hey," I said. She looked up. "Are you this friendly with everybody?"

She smiled sweetly. "Not everybody."

Chapter Seven

My assignment from Harry Schindler was an unfathomable mystery. I spent the days reading his screenplays, a dozen of them, one a day, none of which I cared for. He was a specialist in gangster films and if you looked closely you discovered that all of his scripts were essentially the same, the same plot, the same characters, the same morality. I read them and set them aside. Sometimes I left the office and wandered down the halls. On each office door I saw the nameplate of the famous—Ben Hecht, Tess Slessinger, Dalton Trumbo, Nat West, Horace McCoy, Abem Candel, Frank Edgington. Sometimes I saw these writers entering or leaving their offices. They all looked alike to me. I didn't know them, and they didn't know me. At lunch time one day I went upstairs to the private dining room of the elite, where writers and directors gathered. I took a seat at a long table, and found myself between John Garfield and Rowland Brown, the director. To break the ice I said to Garfield, "Please pass the salt."

He passed it without saying a word. I turned to Brown and asked, "You been here long?"

"Christ, yes," he said, and that was all. It wasn't their fault, I decided. It was I, a social misfit, intimidated, lacking confidence. I never went back there again.

One day walking down the fourth floor corridor I saw a man sitting behind a typewriter in Frank Edgington's office. He was a tall Englishman, smoking a pipe.

I said, "Are you Frank Edgington?"

"That's me."

I crossed to his desk and offered my hand.

"I'm Arturo Bandini. I'm a writer too. I work for Harry Schindler."

"Welcome to the madhouse," Edgington said.

"What are you working on?" I asked.

"A piece of crap. Do you know how to play pick-up-sticks?"

"Sure," I said.

"Want to play a game?"

"Sure."

He took a box of pick-up-stick pieces from his desk and we started to play. Edgington's big bony hands were ill suited for such delicate play. I wasn't any good either. We spent the afternoon at the game, just killing time. Edgington was an Eastern writer. He had contributed to the *New Yorker* and *Scribner's*. He hated Hollywood. He had been in pictures for five years, loathing every moment of it.

"Why don't you leave here?" I asked. "If you hate it so much why don't you go back to New York?"

"Money. I love money."

We went downstairs to the drugstore and ordered cokes.

"Are you married, Edgington?"

"Three times," he said.

"You must like women very much."

"Not anymore. You married?"

"No."

"You're smart. Let's get back to the game."

We returned to his office and played pick-up-sticks until five o'clock.

"Let's have dinner," he said. "Be my guest."

Edgington drove a long black Cadillac. We went to Musso-Frank's. He knew a lot of people, mostly writers. We drank a lot, Edgington putting down scotch, while I drank wine. After dinner and another two hours of liquor we were both pretty drunk. His gray eyes looked at me unsteadily.

"Let's get laid," he said.

"No, I don't need it."

He was suddenly angry, and hammered the table in a

drunken stupor.

"Everybody needs it," he shouted, turning to address people sitting at the surrounding tables. "Let's all get fucked," he shouted.

Three waiters suddenly surrounded our table and hustled us out the back way and into the parking lot. Edgington dropped wearily onto a concrete slab and I sat beside him and lit a cigarette. His face twisted in a sneer.

"God, I hate this town," he said. "Let's get out of here. Let's go to New York."

"I don't want to go to New York, Frank. Take me home."

He staggered to his feet and stumbled toward the car. I didn't like the looks of it.

"Are you sober enough to drive?"

"Get in," he said, "trust me."

He climbed in behind the steering wheel and I circled around to the other door and got in beside him. He bent forward, his face against the steering wheel. I waited a moment, studying him. He began to snore. He was sound asleep. I left him there, quietly slipped out, walked to Hollywood Boulevard, and took a red car to Bunker Hill.

Frank Edgington and I became buddies. He loved the flip side of Hollywood, the bars, the mean streets angling off Hollywood Boulevard to the south. I was glad to tag along as he took in the saloons along El Centro, McCadden Place, Wilcox, and Las Palmas. We drank beer and played the pinball games. Edgington was a pinball addict, a tireless devotee, drinking beer and popping the pinballs. Sometimes we went to the movies. He knew all the fine restaurants, and we ate and drank well. On weekends we toured the Los Angeles basin, the deserts, the foothills, the outlying towns, the harbor. One Saturday we drove to Terminal Island, a strip of white sand in the harbor. The canneries were there and we saw the weatherbeaten beach houses where Filipinos and Japanese lived. It was an enchanting place, lonely, decrepit, picturesque. I saw myself in one of the shacks with my typewriter. I longed for the chance to work there, to write in that lonely, forsaken place, where the sand half covered the streets, and the porches and fences hung limp in the wind. I told Frank I wanted to live there and write there.

"You're crazy," he said. "This is a slum."

"It's beautiful," I said. "It gives me a warm feeling."

At the studio we indulged another of Frank Edgington's obsessions—child games. We played pitch, old maid, Parcheesi, and Chinese checkers. We played for small stakes—five cents a game. When Frank was alone he worked on a short story for the *New Yorker*. When I was alone I sat in my office hungering for Thelma Farber. She was impregnable. Sometimes she even denied me a hello, and I was thoroughly squelched and breathing hard. Harry Schindler ordered his old films and Thelma and I sat in the projection room watching them unroll. I tried to sit next to her and she promptly moved two seats away. She was a bitch, unreasonably hostile. I felt like vermin.

After two weeks I picked up my first paycheck, $600. It was a staggering sum. Three hundred dollars a week for doing nothing! I knocked on Schindler's door and thanked him for the check.

"It's okay," he grinned. "We want you happy. That's the whole idea."

"But I'm not doing anything. I'm going crazy. Give me something to write."

"You're doing fine. I need you in case of emergency. I got to have a backup man, someone with talent. Don't worry about it. You're doing a great job. Keep up the good work. Cash the check and have fun."

"Let me write you a western."

"Not yet," Schindler said. "Just do what you're doing and leave the rest to me."

Suddenly I choked up. I wanted to cry. I turned and walked out, brushed past Thelma and into my office. I sat at my desk crying. I didn't want charity. I wanted to be brilliant on paper, to turn fine phrases and dig up emotional gems for Schindler to see. Choking back my sobs I hurried down the hall to Edgington's office, and flung myself into a chair.

"What the hell's the matter?" Edgington asked.

I told him. "They won't let me write," I said. "Schindler won't assign me anything. I'm going crazy."

Edgington threw his pencil across the room in disgust.

"What the hell's the matter with you? There are writers in this studio who go months without scratching out a line. They earn ten times as much as you do, and they laugh all the way to the bank. Your trouble is that you're a fucking peasant. If there's so much you don't like about this town, stop jerking off and go back to that dago village your people came from. You make my ass tired!"

I stared at him gratefully. Then I began to laugh.

"Frank," I said. "You're a wonderful person."

"Go and sin no more."

I went downstairs to Gower Street, up to Sunset, and across Sunset to the Bank of America, where I cashed my check. I walked out with a new sensation, a feeling of bitter joy. Down Sunset half a block was a used car lot. I found a second-hand Plymouth for $300 and drove away. I was a new person, a successful Hollywood writer, without even writing a line. The future was limitless.

Chapter Eight

A few nights later Edgington invited me to dinner. "Best restaurant in town," he said. We left my car in the studio parking lot and drove off in Frank's Cadillac. He went up Beverly Boulevard to Doheny and pulled into the parking lot of an adjacent restaurant. It was Chasen's. Before we entered Frank straightened my tie.

"This is a high-class joint," he said. "I don't want you to embarrass me."

We walked inside. There was a small outer bar, and beyond that the main dining room. We straddled bar stools and ordered drinks. As usual Frank knew everybody. He shook hands with Dave Chasen and introduced me.

"Nice to know you," Chasen grinned, then turned hastily to welcome a man and two women entering from the street. They stood talking a moment.

Frank nudged me. "Guess who's here," he said.

I turned and studied the man and his two feminine companions.

"Who's he?" I whispered, as the trio moved past and entered the dining room.

"Sinclair Lewis," Frank said.

Startled, I coughed in my drink.

"Are you sure?" I asked.

"Sure I'm sure." He beckoned to Chasen, who joined us again. "Who was the guy with the two women?" Frank asked.

"Sinclair Lewis," Chasen said.

"Good God," I said, "the greatest writer in America!" I leaped off the bar stool and crossed to the curtained door leading to the dining room. Pulling the curtain aside, I saw a waiter ushering Lewis and his friends into a booth.

I couldn't stop myself. All at once I was threading my way between tables toward the greatest author in America. It was a blind, crazy impulse. Suddenly I stood before Lewis's booth. Absorbed in conversation with the women, he did not see me. I smiled at his thinning red hair, his rather freckled face, and his long delicate hands.

"Sinclair Lewis," I said.

He and his friends looked up at me.

"You're the greatest novelist this country ever produced," I spluttered. "All I want is to shake your hand. My name is Arturo Bandini. I write for H. L. Muller, your best friend." I thrust out my hand. "I'm glad to know you, Mr. Lewis."

He fixed me with a bewildered stare, his eyes blue and cold. My hand was out there across the table between us. He did not take it. He only stared, and the women stared too. Slowly I drew my hand away.

"It's nice to know you, Mr. Lewis. Sorry I bothered you." I turned in horror, my guts falling out, as I hurried between the tables and back to the bar, and joined Frank Edgington. I was raging, sick, mortified, humiliated. I snatched Frank's Scotch and soda and gulped it down. The bartender and Frank exchanged glances.

"Give me a pencil and paper, please."

The bartender put a notepad and a pencil before me. Breathing hard, the pencil trembling, I wrote:

Dear Sinclair Lewis:

You were once a god, but now you are a swine. I once reverenced you, admired you, and now you are nothing. I came to shake your hand in adoration, you, Lewis, a giant among American writers, and you rejected it. I swear I shall never read another line of yours again. You are an ill-mannered boor. You have betrayed me. I shall tell H. L. Muller about you, and how you have shamed me. I shall tell the world.

Arturo Bandini

P.S. I hope you choke on your steak.

I folded the paper and signalled a waiter. He walked over. I handed him the note.

"Would you please give this to Sinclair Lewis."

He took it and I gave him some money. He entered the dining room. I stood in the doorway watching him approach Lewis's table. He handed Lewis the note. Lewis held it before him for some moments, then leaped to his feet, looking around, calling the waiter back. He stepped out of the booth and the waiter pointed in my direction. Carrying his napkin, Lewis took big strides as he came toward me. I shot out of there, out the front door, and down the street to the parking lot, to Frank's Cadillac, and leaped into the back seat. I could see the street from where I sat, and in a moment Lewis appeared nervously on the sidewalk, still clutching his napkin. He glanced about, agitated.

"Bandini," he called. "Where are you? I'm Sinclair Lewis. Where are you, Bandini?"

I sat motionless. A few moments, and he walked back toward the restaurant. I sat back, exhausted, bewildered, not knowing myself, or my capabilities. I sat with doubts, with shame, with torment, with regret. I lit a cigarette and sucked it greedily. In a little while Frank Edgington walked out of the restaurant and came to the car. He leaned inside and looked at me.

"You okay?"

"Okay," I said.

"What happened?"

"I don't know."

"What was that note you wrote?"

"I don't know."

"You're crazy. You want to eat?"

"Not here. Let's go someplace else."

"It's up to you." He got behind the wheel and started the engine.

Chapter Nine

I was born in a basement apartment of a macaroni factory in North Denver. When my father learned that his third child was also a son he reacted in the same fashion as when my two brothers came into the world—he got drunk for three days. My mother found him in the back room of a saloon down the street from our apartment and dragged him home. Beyond that my father paid little attention to me.

One day in my infancy I stood outside the bathroom window of my aunt's house and watched my cousin Catherine standing before the dresser mirror combing out her long red hair. She was stark naked except for her mother's high-heeled shoes, a full-fledged woman of eight years. I did not understand the ecstasy that boiled up in me, the confusion of my cousin's electric beauty pouring into me. I stood there and masturbated. I was five years old and the world had a new and staggering dimension.

I was also a criminal. I felt like a criminal, a skulking, snot-nosed, freckle-faced, inscrutable criminal for four years thereafter, until sagging beneath the weight of my cross, I dragged myself into my first confession and told the priest the truth of my bestial life. He gave me absolution and I flung away the heavy cross and walked out into the sunlight, a free soul again.

Our family moved to Boulder when I was seven and my two brothers and I attended Sacred Heart School. During the ensuing eight years I achieved high marks in baseball, basketball and football, and my life was not cluttered with books or scholarship.

My father, a building contractor, prospered for a while in Boulder and sent me to a Jesuit high school. Most of the time I was miserable there. I got fair marks but chafed at the discipline. I hated boarding school and longed to be home, but my marks were fair and after four years I enrolled in the University of Colorado. During my second year at the university I fell in love with a girl who worked in a clothing store. Her name was Agnes, and I wanted to marry her. She moved to North Platte, Nebraska, for a better job, and I quit the university to be near her. I hitchhiked from Boulder to North Platte and arrived dusty and broke and triumphant at the rooming house where Agnes lived. We sat on the porch swing and she was not glad to see me.

"I don't want to marry you," she said. "I don't want to see you any more. That's why I'm here, so we don't see each other."

"I'll get a job," I insisted. "We'll have a family."

"Oh for Christ's sake."

"Don't you want a family? Don't you like kids?"

She got quickly to her feet. "Go home, Arturo. Please go home. Don't think about me any more. Go back to school. Learn something." She was crying.

"I can lay brick," I said, moving to her. She threw her arms around me, and planted a wet kiss on my cheek, then pushed me away.

"Go home, Arturo. Please." She went inside and closed the door.

I walked down to the railroad tracks and swung aboard a freight train bound for Denver. From there I took another freight to Boulder and home. The next day I went to the job where my father was laying brick.

"I want to talk to you," I said. He came down from the scaffold and we walked to a pile of lumber.

"What's the matter?" he said.

"I quit school."

"Why?"

"I'm not cut out for it."

His face twisted bitterly. "What are you going to do now?"

"I don't know. I haven't figured it out."

"Jesus, you're crazy."

I became a bum in my home town. I loafed around. I took a job pulling weeds, but it was hard and I quit. Another job, washing windows. I barely got through it. I looked all over Boulder for work, but the streets were full of young, unemployed men. The only job in town was delivering newspapers. It paid fifty cents a day. I turned it down. I leaned against walls in the pool halls. I stayed away from home. I was ashamed to eat the food my father and mother provided. I always waited until my father walked out. My mother tried to cheer me. She made me pecan pie and ravioli.

"Don't worry," she said. "You wait and see. Something will happen. It's in my prayers."

I went to the library. I looked at the magazines, at the pictures in them. One day I went to the bookshelves, and pulled out a book. It was *Winesburg, Ohio*. I sat at a long mahogany table and began to read. All at once my world turned over. The sky fell in. The book held me. The tears came. My heart beat fast. I read until my eyes burned. I took the book home. I read another Anderson. I read and I read, and I was heartsick and lonely and in love with a book, many books, until it came naturally, and I sat there with a pencil and a long tablet, and tried to write, until I felt I could not go on because the words would not come as they did in Anderson, they only came like drops of blood from my heart.

Chapter Ten

Not a week passed without a letter from my mother. Written on lined grade-school paper they reflected her fears, her hopes, her anxiety, and her curious view of what went on in the world. They bothered me, those letters. Their phrasing fluttered in my head like trapped birds, flapping about at the most inopportune times. Often I simply laughed at them, other times they angered and frustrated me and I pitied my poor innocent mother:

> Be careful, Arturo. Say your prayers. Remember that one Hail Mary to the Virgin Mary will get you anything. Wear your scapular medal. It was blessed by Father Agatha, a very holy man. Thank God you all have one. . . .

Joe Santucci, my high school buddy next door, had completed a tour in the navy and was now back in Boulder again. My mother wrote:

> Poor Mrs. Santucci. Her boy is back after three years and he is a communist. She asked me to pray for him. Such a nice boy. I talked to him this morning and I couldn't believe he was a communist. He seems just the same. . . .

> Please send us some money when you can. Our grocery bill is $390. I pay cash now, but there isn't enough and your father hasn't worked for two weeks. . . .

I miss you all the time. I found a pair of your socks with holes in them, and darned them and started to cry. Say your prayers. I went to mass this morning and offered communion for your good luck. . . .

Joe Santucci told Papa about Los Angeles. He says the women are bad and all over and there are saloons every place. Wear your scapular medal for protection. Go to mass, try to meet some nice Catholic girls. . . .

I am glad you are working in the restaurant, and the other job with the writer. Send me some money if you can. Your father hurt his hand and can't work for a while. We miss you. Try a novena. Nobody ever said a novena without getting help. . . .

I sent her $200 from my first studio paycheck and eventually paid off the grocery bill.

Chapter Eleven

Mrs. Brownell and I were experiencing some turbulence. She had doubts about my working in the studio, and was careful not to question me about it. We were silent together during long periods, and it was difficult to invent small talk. Sitting before the radio we listened to Jack Benny and Bob Hope and Fred Allen until it was time to go to bed. We lay in the darkness and stared at the ceiling until sleep came. I felt far away from her, a drifting away as the strangeness developed. She was cold and silent in the morning, the gap widening. It was coming, and I knew it, a separation, a break. I told myself I didn't care. I was working, I had money. I didn't have to stay in that ancient hotel. I could move to Hollywood now, into the Hollywood hills. I could rent my own house and even hire a cleaning woman. Bunker Hill was not forever. A man had to move on.

Thinking of her depressed me. I sat in my office and squirmed, thinking how old she was, five years older than my own mother, and I gagged, and tried to cough away the unpleasantness. I thought of her face, the little lines around her eyes, the cables in her neck, the crinkled skin of her arms, her old body, the buttocks too small, her dresses too long, the crack of her knees when she sat down, her sunken cheeks when she removed her dentures, her cold feet, her old Kansas ways. I didn't need it, I told myself. I had only to turn my back to make it go away. I could have any girl in town, any starlet, maybe even a star. All I had to do was apply myself. It was wrong to spend my best years with an old woman who gave me only old thoughts in return. I needed a bright and lovely creature familiar with the arts, steeped in literature, someone who loved Keats and Rupert Brooke and Ernest Dowson. Not a woman who got her literary inspiration from her hometown Kansas newspaper. She had befriended me, yes, she had been kind to me, yes, but I had been kind to her too. I had given my juices to her, served as her friend and companion. Now it was time to move on.

I looked around my office and sighed. I loved it all. I was born to it. Maybe I wasn't writing a line, but I had found my station. I was making good money and the future was limitless. I had to get away from that woman.

All morning I sat brooding in gloom, for it was ever thus with me, probing the ashes, searching for blemishes, overwhelmed in despair. At noon she telephoned, and my heart leaped and I was glad.

"Still mad?" she asked.

"No. And you?"

"No," she said, "I'm so sorry. I don't know what got into me."

"It wasn't your fault. I did it. I don't know why. I never know why. It's for you to forgive me."

"I do, I do. You're a sweet boy. You're good for me. We mustn't quarrel."

"Never again. Let's have some fun. Let's celebrate."

"I'd love that. Let's do something crazy."

"How about a good dinner first?"

"I'll wear my new suit."

"I've got a new suit too."

"Wear it."

"I love you," I said. "You're the dearest woman in the world. We'll have a party."

She wasn't there when I returned to the hotel at six o'clock. There was a note for me on the desk. Back in a moment, it said. I walked back to my room, showered, and got into my new suit. I had never worn it before. A fine, hand-tailored $200 job. I studied myself in the mirror. The reflection was perfect: a high-priced writer. The shoulders were padded a little more than I wanted, but it was a pleasant garment. We belonged together. I walked down the hall to the lobby and she was there behind the desk, beaming as I kissed her. There was a scarf over her hair. She withdrew it and primped.

"Like it?" she asked. "It's a pageboy."

Her graying hair had been turned under at the ends in a sleek roll. It was stiff from the beauty parlor. I studied it but could not conjure up an opinion.

"Great," I said. "Fine."

I noticed a touch of rouge on her cheeks. It seemed superfluous.

"Where are we going?" she asked.

"First we're going to Rene and Jean's."

"Lovely," she said. "Let's have a cocktail."

We walked into her apartment, and there were two martinis on the table. I lifted one and toasted her:

"To the kindest, sweetest girl in all the world."

She smiled and sipped her drink. It made her cough and she laughed. While she dressed I sat down and had a couple more. She was in the bathroom for a long time. When she emerged, playfully stilted as if modelling, she showed off her Joan Crawford suit with wide shoulders and narrow skirt. She was taller, in high-heeled ankle-strap shoes. I felt a shudder of lust and kissed her. There was a thin film of scarlet lip rouge on her mouth. Perhaps it was too much. I didn't know. It made me wonder.

We took my car and drove out Wilshire to Vermont and parked in Rene and Jean's lot. We had been to the restaurant frequently and it was a pleasure to be greeted by old Jean and the waiters. We drank wine and ate too much. When it was time to leave she asked, "Where to now?"

I was ready for it. "Leave that to me."

We drove back to Wilshire and turned toward the Ambassador Hotel. She was quiet and smiling and a little frowsy. Leaning back against the seat, the wide shoulders of her tailored suit had lost their elegance and seemed to overdress her. At the Ambassador I turned into the driveway, and parked the car and got out. She stepped from the car and looked about mystified. I took her arm.

"Let's go," I said, leading her toward the hotel.

"Where are we going?" she asked.

"To the Coconut Grove and the music of Anson Weeks."

She squealed and hugged my arm in delight. "It's so nice to be with a famous writer!"

"Not famous, but working."

We walked to the hotel entrance.

"My feet hurt," she whispered.

The strains of Anson Weeks' music wafted from the ballroom as we entered the lobby. The song was "Where the Blue of the Night Meets the Gold of the Day." I held her arm and could feel the beat of her heart.

"I'm so happy," she said. "I always wanted to come to the Coconut Grove and here I am."

The headwaiter greeted us and bowed, "Good evening."

I nodded. "We'd like a table."

He led us into the big resplendent room with its colored lights and coconut trees. On the dance floor couples glided to the music, and spotlights played colored beams over the walls and ceiling. Our table was on the second tier. We sat down.

"Would you like a cocktail now?" the waiter asked.

Mrs. Brownell was so breathless that she could only nod in assent.

"I'll have a brandy," I said.

She put her hand on mine across the table. "I'll have one too," she said.

The waiter disappeared. We watched the dancers.

"I can't dance," I said. "At least, not very well."

She squeezed my hand again. "I'll teach you."

I started to rise. "Let's try it."

"Not now," she breathed. "Let's wait a dance or two."

Then the waiter returned with our drinks. He put my brandy before me and smiled as he served Mrs. Brownell.

"Here you are, mother," he said.

It cut her like a knife. Her startled eyes fixed me. They seemed guilt stricken, embarrassed, intimidated. She lowered her head and I thought she was going to cry. But she did not cry. She lifted her face and smiled bravely. The embarrassed waiter moved off.

"Drink your brandy," I urged.

She sipped carefully and our attention went back to the dancers.

What happened thereafter was my effort to make a joke, to cheer her, to make light of the waiter's gaffe. The band began to play a Strauss waltz. Then I said it.

"Shall we dance, mother dear?"

She looked frightened, biting her lip and staring helplessly at me, her eyes suddenly awash with tears. Crying uncontrollably, she shook the table as she groped to her feet and rushed away toward the lobby. I downed my brandy and hurried after her. She was not in the lobby nor on the staircase, and I stepped outside in time to see a cab pulling out of the driveway with Mrs. Brownell in the back seat. I ran after her calling, but the cab sped away. I walked back to the Grove, paid my bill, and went out to my car.

What a mess. I drove back to the hotel reluctantly. I hated facing her, her tears, but it had to be. I turned the key in her apartment door and walked inside. There was a hiss of water from the shower in the bathroom. Sprawled on the floor, wantonly discarded, was her Joan Crawford suit, as if dropped from her body and kicked aside. Her blouse hung over a chair, her shoes and stockings carelessly discarded.

I undressed down to my shorts, and slipped between the covers of the studio couch, folding my arms behind my head, waiting for her to appear. I had nothing to say. I decided to leave it up to her. She emerged finally, dressed in her nightie, my unexpected presence irritating her. She had washed her hair, washed out her coiffure, and her hair hung in moist strands. Her face was scrubbed and plain and wrinkled.

"Please go," she said.

"I'm sorry."

She crossed to the window and flung it open. The cool of the night wafted in from the hillside. Without a word she gathered up my clothes, my coat and pants, my shirt, my shoes. At first I thought she was tidying up. Instead she turned to the window and flung everything out into the night. I leaped out of bed and rushed to the window. Below I saw my clothes flung about on the weed-clogged terrain. It was a steep incline. My scattered garments looked like dead bodies. My pants hung from the branch of a tree. I glared at her.

"Satisfied?"

"Not until you leave."

I started to gather up her garments—the Crawford suit, the blouse, the underskirt. She rushed to stop me, and we struggled, pushing and pulling, but I was the stronger, and broke her grasp, and flung her things through the window. With a smile I said, "I'll go now."

"And don't come back," she panted. I walked down the hall to my room, put on a robe and slippers and moved down to a door at the rear of the hotel, which opened on the yard area. As I scrambled up the hillside to my clothes I saw Mrs. Brownell making her way down the hillside. We glared at one another and began gathering our things. I had to climb the tree to reach my pants. When I dropped to the ground she was crawling back toward the hotel front. At my feet was one of her shoes. I picked it up and threw it. The shoe hit her in the ass. Enraged, she picked it up and hurled it down at me. It sailed over my head.

I was very sad when I got back to my room. Women! I knew nothing about women. There was no understanding them. I opened a suitcase and dumped my things into it. The room spoke to me, and implored me to stay—the Maxfield Parrish picture on the wall, the typewriter on the table, my bed, my marvellous bed, the window overlooking the hill, the source of so many dreams, so many thoughts, so many words, a part of myself, the echo of myself pleading with me to stay. I didn't want to go but there was no denying it, I had somehow blundered and kicked myself out, and there was no turning back. Goodbye to Bunker Hill.

Chapter Twelve

When Frank Edgington learned that I was homeless he invited me to his house in the hills above Beechwood Drive. It was a two-bedroom place in a thicket of eucalyptus. He showed me to my bedroom, and I put my suitcase on the bare floor. There was no bed in the room—except for a double mattress pushed against the wall.

Living with Edgington was a strange experience. His style emerged out of his childhood, and the games we played in his office were as nothing compared to the games scattered about in his living room. We plunged into the glamorous, romantic, enthralling life in Hollywood, beginning with a game of ping pong in the garage. Then we moved to the kitchen and filled our tumblers with table wine. On to the living room, throwing ourselves on the parquet floor, and thrilling to a game of tiddlywinks. The more we drank the wilder we played. We battled one another at the dart board. Sometimes we fell asleep playing bingo. It was pure and it was clean and when it rained and water thundered on the roof we turned on the gaslight in the fireplace and it was like turning back to a boyhood time beside a campfire in the mountains.

I rarely saw my boss Harry Schindler. When I ran into him in the elevator or down the hall he grabbed my arm affectionately and steered me along.

"How's it going?"

"Okay," I'd answer, "just fine."

"You're doing a hell of a job. Keep it up."

"I'm not writing, Harry. I want to write."

"Hang in there. Take your time. Let me worry about your writing."

Every day the reception room we shared was full of mysterious people waiting to see him. They must have been writers, directors, production people. When I asked my secretary who they were she wouldn't tell me. As time went by I felt like an orphan, a pariah, non-productive, unknown and exiled. The money kept me there, the absence of poverty, the fear of its return. The thought of being a busboy again made me shiver. I took out my little savings account passbook and studied the figures. I was up to $1,800, and still sending money home. I had no cause for complaint.

One morning Thelma knocked on my door and opened it.

"Harry wants to see you."

I found Schindler lighting a fresh cigar.

"I may have something for you pretty soon," he said. I got excited.

"You mean an assignment?"

"Maybe. We're negotiating."

"What is it?"

"A novel, *The Genius*, by Theodore Dreiser."

"Oh my God! When will you know?"

"A couple of weeks."

I left his office in a dream. Thelma studied my face. I bent down and kissed her on the mouth.

"Get me a copy of *The Genius* by Theodore Dreiser." The novel came up from the studio library within the hour, and I began to read. It was a very long novel and by the end of the week I had read it twice and collected a notebook of ideas on how to convert it into a picture.

Two months later I read *The Genius* for what must have been the tenth time and I had four notebooks filled with observations, stacked on my desk. I jumped whenever the phone rang, thinking it was Schindler. I kept my door open watching the reception room for his appearance. His office had another door leading to the hall. Whenever I heard it open I jumped up and rushed outside. A couple of times I stood waiting as he appeared. It was as if he did not see me at all as he walked by. I slunk back to my office and sat brooding.

Why was he doing this? What was happening to me? Was there some conspiracy against me in the world? Had I offended him? Hadn't he offered me this job? Was I accursed by Almighty God? Perhaps my mother was right. Lose your faith and you lose all. Was she better informed than I on the ways of the Lord? Was I too late to make amends? I walked down to the parking lot, got in my car, and drove up Sunset to the Catholic church. Kneeling in the front pew, I prayed:

"Please, God, do something about that assignment. I haven't asked anything of you for years. Do this for me and I will come back into the arms of Mother Church for the rest of my days."

After a while a priest appeared and moved into the confessional. A few old women knelt in the vicinity. I went to kneel with them. Then it was my turn and I entered the confessional. Through the wooden grillwork I saw the priest's white face. I had nothing to say. The guilt for past sins had left me. I knelt there in embarrassment. The moments passed. The priest stirred. His eyes sought mine through the grill.

"Yes?" he asked.

"I'm sorry," I whispered, "I haven't prepared myself." I rose and walked out, down the aisle and through the heavy front doors to the street. I was more despondent than ever, for somewhere in my heart there had always been a conviction that the church was my ace in the hole. I had always believed this without articulating it. Now the conviction was gone and I was lost, and facing a hostile world. I walked down to my car and got in. Suddenly, desperately, I got out again and hurried back into the church and knelt down and tried to pray.

I murmured a Hail Mary and found it interrupted by Thelma Farber. Hail Mary full of grace and Thelma Farber naked in my arms. Holy Mary, Mother of God, kissing Thelma Farber's breasts, groping at her body and running my hands along her thighs. Pray for us sinners now and at the hour of our death and my lips moved to Thelma's loins and I kissed her ecstatically. I was lost, writhing. I felt my body kneeling there, the hardness in my loins, the fullness of an erection, the absurdity of it, the maddening dichotomy. I arose and dashed out of there, down to my car, and drove off, frightened, shaking, absurd.

I was glad when I got back to my office. It was like a nest that comforted me. Thelma was not there. I closed the door, sat at my desk and lit a cigarette. Mysterious unsettling things were happening to me. I had stepped out of the world and now it was hard to find my way back. I thought of Frank Edgington down the hall. Perhaps I could tell him my problem. But that was no good. Edgington was too sardonic, too impatient. He would merely laugh and blame it on my peasant origin.

There was a knock on the door. It was Thelma. A few minutes ago I had knelt in the church and kissed her loins and there she was again. She sensed something.

"You okay?" she asked.

"Sure."

"Harry wants to see you."

"What about?"

"How should I know?"

I crossed the reception room to Schindler's door and knocked.

"Come in."

I opened the door and found him sitting there.

"You wanted to see me?"

"Bad news."

I moved closer.

"We can't buy the Dreiser book," he said.

"Why not?"

"It's not for sale." Somehow it didn't seem important.

"What now?" I asked.

"Continue what you're doing."

"I have pages and pages of notes on Dreiser's book. Do you want to see them?"

"No," he said, "forget it."

"Give me something to write."

"I don't have anything."

I felt rage. "Think of something, you bastard!"

He looked at me with a tight jaw, and got slowly to his feet.

"Get out of here."

I turned and walked out, back to my office. I felt it then, my grief, the rim of the world, the loneliness of being far away and lost, and I was crying. I threw myself on the studio couch and let myself go, sobbing. Thelma came to the door. She spoke softly.

"Arturo, what is it?"

I sat up and told her what Schindler had said, and started crying again.

"You poor thing!" She moved to the couch and sat down. I felt the weight of her body sinking upon the couch. It felt good. Encouraged, I sobbed again. She put her long soft arm around my shoulder and dabbed my eyes with her handkerchief. It was scented with her fragrance. I turned toward her and put my head on her shoulder. She hugged me gently.

"Help me, Thelma," I said. "I'm so unhappy."

She dabbed my wet eyes and pulled me closer, her bosom pressed against mine.

"Oh, Thelma, help me!"

"There, there," she soothed, stroking my hair.

"Oh, Thelma, kiss me!"

She rose, went to the door and closed it, then returned to sit beside me again.

"Oh, Thelma. If you only knew how I've hungered for you, how I've wanted to hold you in my arms, to kiss you."

"I've guessed it," she said. "The way you've looked at me, I've known all the time."

I lay back on the couch and pulled her toward me, her mouth settled on mine, soft and cool and full. Suddenly I groped at my fly, and tugged at the zipper, while she stood up and lifted her skirt and pulled down her white panties. She sank to the floor and spread her limbs.

"Hurry," she breathed.

I rolled off the couch and positioned myself between her long smooth stockinged legs, but the zipper gave me trouble still, and I fought it desperately. Her hands probed at my belt and in one violent jerk my pants were down. I bent over her, my shooter at the ready as I sought to spear her, but I missed, and missed again, and with a little cry of annoyance she grabbed the thing and tried to insert it, and at that moment I heard the click of the doorknob and the sound of the door opening, and I rolled my eyes toward the door and saw Harry Schindler looking down at us. The life went out of the shooter, and I could do no more than lie there stupified while Thelma lay shocked, holding the limp thing in one hand.

"All right, Thelma," Schindler said quietly. "Put that mushroom down, and get the hell out of here."

She arose, straightened her dress, and looked at him in contempt and defiance, striding past him and out of the room, her panties in one hand.

"I'll see you later!" he threatened. She tossed her head defiantly.

I got to my feet and pulled up my trousers.

"Let's talk," Schindler said. He turned and walked out.

I found him waiting for me, his feet on the desk, a new cigar in his mouth. He looked at me with a smirk.

"I can't believe it," he said. "It's not possible."

"I'm sorry, Harry."

"Sorry for what? It wasn't your fault. It never is."

"But it was. I seduced her."

He dropped his feet to the floor and leaned forward.

"Listen, kid. She eats writers alive. I mean big writers, Pulitzer prize winners, academy award writers, $3,000-a-week writers. That's what I don't understand. You! You don't even have a screen credit!"

I didn't know whether he was complimenting me or not.

"It just happened," I said. "I hardly expected it. But don't hold it against her. I mean don't fire her."

"I'm firing you," Schindler said. "As of now, you're

through."

"What about Thelma? Is she fired too?"

"I can't fire her. I'll never fire her. I want her around so I can keep an eye on her, but I'll tell you this—if it happens again I'll divorce her."

I said, "Oh God, Schindler," and walked out in a daze.

Chapter Thirteen

You had to have an agent. Without one you were an outcast, an unknown. Having an agent gave you status, even if he never delivered. When one writer said to another, "Who's your agent?" and you answered, "I don't have any," he immediately surmised that you lacked talent. Edgington's agent was Cyril Korn.

"You won't like him," Edgington warned, "but he's good."

I sent three magazine stories to Korn's office in Beverly Hills, and waited for his telephone call.

It never came. Finally, Edgington phoned him and made an appointment for me. His office was in a new building on Beverly Drive. His secretary announced me and I sat down to wait. After two hours I was admitted to the great man's office.

He stood in the middle of his carpeted room, tapping golf balls into a glass. He didn't even say hello. Finally, stroking his putter with great concentration, he spoke without looking at me.

"I read your short stories," he said.

"Did you like them?"

"Hated them. You got no chance trying to peddle that kind of trash in pictures."

"I'm not trying to peddle them in pictures. I just wanted to prove that I can write."

He put away the putter, and looked at me for the first time. "I don't think you can."

"You mean you don't want to handle me?"

"Have you written any screenplays?"

"No, but I've written a treatment for Harry Schindler. I did Dreiser's *The Genius.*"

"And he fired you. Have you ever collaborated with anybody?"

"No."

"I have a client who needs a collaborator—somebody who's young and unsophisticated and unspoiled. My client's name is Velda van der Zee. Ever heard of her?"

"Never have."

"Where you been all these years? Velda van der Zee has written more screenplays than you'll ever write in three life times."

"You think we'd work well together?"

"It's a big opportunity for you. Maybe you'll get a screen credit."

"I'd like to try."

"I'll let you know." The phone rang. Korn picked it up and gestured to me with a wave of his hand. It meant: get out. I left in disgust. He had put me down and insulted me and filled me with misery, and I wanted no part of him. All the way home I ground my teeth when I thought of him standing there in a red velvet vest putting golf balls. I would rather get out of the business than have him for my agent. I would rather sling hash in Abe Marx's deli than have him represent me. When I told Edgington about our meeting he smiled quietly.

"He's peculiar, but he's a good agent. Wait and see what happens."

"I won't even talk to the sonofabitch."

Next morning the Cyril Korn office telephoned. It was the secretary: "Mr. Korn would like to see you at two o'clock this afternoon." She hung up.

At two o'clock I sat in Korn's office waiting. At four, after one pack of cigarettes, I was admitted.

There was Cyril Korn behind his desk, red vest and all, talking to a woman seated across from him. She was a large, florid woman, with melonlike breasts, wearing a big hat and bouncing earrings. Her makeup was heavy, her lips too red. She smiled at me.

"Velda," Korn said, "I want you to meet Arturo Bandini. He says he's a writer."

Velda held out her jewelled hand and I shook it. "It's nice to know you," I said.

"A pleasure," she answered.

Korn rose. "I'll leave you two for a while," he said. "I want you to read something. He lifted a couple of manuscripts from his desk and handed one to each of us. "Read this and tell me what you think. I'll be back in an hour." He left the office and closed the door.

"You *are* young, aren't you?" Velda said.

"I may be young but I'm a hell of a writer."

She laughed. Her teeth were false. "You know something?" she said. "You look like Spencer Tracy. I saw Spence this morning at Musso-Frank's. We had breakfast together. He was telling me about working with Loretta Young—how he loved it. She's really gorgeous, don't you think? I know Loretta and Sally and their mother. Such a lovely family. She was under contract at Metro when I was out there. We used to have lunch together, Loretta and I and Carole Lombard and Joan Crawford. You'd love Joan. Such a fine figure of a woman. And Robert Taylor! I swear he's the handsomest man in Hollywood, excluding Clark Gable, of course. Clark and I are old friends. I knew him when he first started in the business. I've seen him scale the heights, and look at him now! They say he's in love with Claudette Colbert, but I don't believe it. I saw him at the tennis club the other day and asked him if it was true. He laughed that merry masculine laugh of his, and kissed me on the cheek and said, 'You want the truth, Velda? I'm in love with you.' Wasn't that priceless? John Barrymore always said the same thing to me. Such a tease! Not at all like Lionel or Ethel, but a free spirit, a romantic poem of a man. Some people say that Errol Flynn is more handsome, but I can't believe it. Ronald Coleman, though, he's something else—so dashing, with sparkling eyes, and princely manners. He gave a party a couple of weeks ago in Santa Barbara. It had to be the most wonderful soirée in Hollywood history. Norma Shearer was there, and Tallulah Bankhead and Alice Faye and Jean Harlow and Wallace Beery and Richard Barthelmess and Harold Lloyd and Douglas Fairbanks, Jr. Oh, it was fabulous—a night I'll never forget!"

She paused for breath. "But here I am talking about myself as usual. Tell me, do you like Hollywood?"

"Sometimes yes," I said, "and sometimes no."

"Isn't that funny!" she exclaimed. "Pat O'Brien said the same thing to me last week at Warner Brothers. We were having lunch in the Green Room at Warner Brothers—Pat and I and Bette Davis and Glenda Farrell. I don't know why we got on the subject of Hollywood, but Pat looked very reflective and said exactly what you've just said."

The door opened and Cyril Korn returned. "How are you two getting along?" he asked.

"Just fine," Velda van der Zee said. "We're going to make a great team."

He turned to me. "You like the story?" he asked.

"Of course he does," Velda said. "He's in love with it, aren't you, Arturo?"

"I guess so."

Korn clapped his hands. "Then it's settled. I'll call Jack Arthur and tell him it's a deal."

"Who's Jack Arthur?" I asked. Before he could answer Velda said:

"Jack Arthur happens to be one of the most delightful producers in Hollywood. He's been my close friend for ten years. I was a bridesmaid at his wedding, and the godmother of his two children. Need I say more?"

"No," I said. "That's fine, fine."

One thing about Cyril Korn: When he wanted you to leave he almost threw you out. He returned to his desk and sat down. "That's it, kids. I'll be in touch."

I walked out with Velda. We descended the elevator to the street floor and walked out on the parking lot.

"Do you know anything about Indian wrestling?" she

asked.

"Not much," I said.

"Last night at Jeannette McDonald's house, Lewis Stone and Frank Morgan tried their hands at Indian wrestling. It was a scream. They tugged and pushed until the sweat broke out on their faces. And do you know who won?"

"Who?"

"Lewis Stone!" she exclaimed. "That fine elderly gentleman defeated Frank Morgan at Indian wrestling. Everybody screamed with laughter and applauded."

I glanced at her. Her round face was flushed with excitement. Words tumbled from her lips, unstoppable. No doubt about it, she was a dingbat. She lived in a world of names, not bodies, not human beings, but famous names. Nothing she said could possibly be true. She simply invented as she prattled on. She was a liar, a lovable liar, her mind bubbling with preposterous tales.

She led me to her car—a bronze-colored Bentley.

"Wow!" I said. She beamed at her sleek car.

"It looks expensive," I said. That pleased her.

"I bought it from Wallace Beery," she said. "Wally decided on a Rolls Royce, and I got it for a bargain."

She threw open the rear door and I peered inside. The seat was green velour. There was a stain in the middle, a brown stain. She smiled.

"You're looking at that brown spot, aren't you? Claire Dodd did it. I took her home from a party at Jeannettte McDonald's and she spilled a glass of wine on it. Poor Claire! So humiliated! She wanted to pay for getting it cleaned, but I wouldn't have it. After all, what are friends for?"

"Do you want me to call you?" I asked. She gave me her telephone number, and we shook hands.

"Can I give you a ride?"

"I have a car," I said, nodding toward my Plymouth.

"Isn't that a Ford?" she asked.

"Almost," I said. "It's a Plymouth."

"I used to own one. They're very uncomfortable."

We said goodbye and I walked to my uncomfortable car.

The script Cyril Korn had given us was by Harry Browne. It was the story of a range war—the struggle between cattle men and sheep men. The cattle men were the bad guys and the sheep men the good guys. Also featured was a tribe of hostile Indians who captured Julia, the heroine, and imprisoned her in the Indian village. When the sheep men and the cattle men learn of her capture they join forces and ride off to rescue Julia. After the battle in which Julia is saved, the cattle men and sheep men shake hands and the range war is brought to a peaceful solution.

A couple of days later Velda van der Zee and I drove the Bentley out Ventura to Liberty Studios to meet the producer, Jack Arthur. I sat beside her as she handled the quiet magnificent machine. She liked the story, she said. It was a classic, a sure nominee for the academy awards. She visualized Gary Cooper and Claire Trevor in the leading roles, with Jack La Rue playing the part of Magua, the Indian chief.

"Gary Cooper's a friend of mine," she said. "I'll give him the screenplay. He has a high regard for my opinion."

"Sounds good," I said.

We pulled into the parking lot at Liberty Studios and walked down the hall to Jack Arthur's office. Jack Arthur was a pipe smoker. He kissed Velda on the cheek and shook my hand.

"Well," he said, "what do you think of the story?"

"Priceless," Velda said. "We love it."

"It has possibilities," Arthur said. "Are you ready to go to work?"

"Of course," Velda said. "How are the children?"

"They're fine, fine."

"You must meet Jack's children, Arturo. They're the most delightful creatures in the world."

Jack Arthur beamed. "You'll need an office," he said, reaching for the telephone.

Quickly Velda said, "That won't be necessary. We'll

- 82 -

work at my house." She turned to me and smiled. "Is that all right with you, Arturo?"

"Fine, fine," I said.

"Okay, then," Arthur said. "I'll get in touch with Cyril Korn and we'll draw up the contracts. You people need anything, just holler." He shook my hand. "Good luck, Bandini. Write me a smash hit."

"I'll try." Velda and I said goodbye and left.

On the way back to town I said, "I didn't know we were going to work at your place."

"I always work there."

"Where do you live?"

"In Benedict Canyon. William Powell's old house. You'll love it." She began to speak of Irene Dunne and Myrna Loy, but I was used to it by now and scarcely heard her as she moved on to Lew Ayres, Frederic March, Jean Harlow and Mary Astor. When she pulled up in front of Frank Edgington's house she was well into a reminiscence of Franchot Tone, and I had to sit there patiently until the tale was told. Then I stepped out and she drove away.

The next day I drove out Benedict Canyon to Velda van der Zee's French chateau. It was nestled in a grove of birch trees, white and serene and aristocratic. Twin towers with slate roofs guarded the front entrance, and a great oak door stood between Doric columns. A housekeeper answered the summons of the lion's-head knocker. She was a middle-aged black woman in a maid's costume.

"I'm Arturo Bandini."

"I know," she smiled. "Please come in."

I followed her through an entry hall and into the living room. The place was awesome, intimidating, crowded with Louis Quinze furniture and huge beaded lamps. Over the mantel hung the large oil portrait of an elderly man with a white beard and mustache.

"Who's that?" I asked.

"Mr. van der Zee," the maid said.

"I guess I've never met him."

"You can't," the maid said. "He's dead."

"He must have been very rich," I said.

She laughed. "You'd be rich too if you owned half of Signal Hill."

"Oh."

Down the grand staircase came Velda van der Zee, afloat in a diaphanous hostess gown. Silken panels floated behind her like attendant cherubs, and a cloud of exotic perfume enveloped me as she offered her hand.

"Good morning, Arturo. Shall we go to work, or would you like to see the rest of the house?"

"Let's work," I said.

She took my arm. "That's what I like about you, young man, your dedication." She guided me into an eerie room.

"This is my den," she said.

I looked around. It was indeed a den. Every inch of wallspace was crowded with autographed photos of film stars. The beautiful people. So handsome, so full of buoyant smiles and glittering teeth and graceful hands and beautiful skins. But it was a sad room too, a kind of mausoleum, a display of the living and the dead. Velda looked at them reverently.

"My beloved friends," she sighed.

I wanted to ask about her husband, but it seemed inappropriate. She crossed to an elaborate French provincial desk, a typewriter upon it.

"My favorite desk," she said. "A Christmas present from Maurice Chevalier."

"It's a beauty," I said.

Velda pulled a red bellcord beside the doorway. A bell rang and the maid appeared. Velda ordered coffee. I went to the desk and sat before the typewriter.

"Have you read the script?" I asked.

"Not yet. I plan to do it this morning."

She crossed to a divan and sat down.

"Shall I tell you something very interesting about this room?"

"Please do."

"This is where I signed my first contract with Louis B.

Mayer. He sat exactly where you are and signed the papers. That was ten years ago. He's a wonderful man. One of these days we'll have a party and you can meet him. If he likes you your future is assured."

"I'd love to meet him." I pulled the script from my coat pocket. "Let's get started."

The maid entered with a coffee tray. Velda talked as she poured. "Lots of famous people have graced this room throughout the years. Do you remember Vilma Banky and Rod La Roque?"

That started her off. Vilma Banky, Rod La Roque, Clara Bow, Lillian Gish, Marian Davies, John Gilbert, Colleen Moore, Clive Brooke, Buster Keaton, Harold Lloyd, Wesley Barry, Billie Dove, Corinne Griffith, Claire Windsor. On and on she sailed through clouds of reverie, sipping coffee, lighting cigarettes, dreaming the absurd, invoking the glamour of enchanting lies and impossible worlds she had made for herself.

I sat listening in quiet despair, thinking of ways to escape, to run out of there, to leap into my car and drive back to the reality of Bunker Hill, to scream, to jump up and scream, to beg her to shut up, and then finally to give in and sink mortally wounded into the big chair that once held Louis B.'s ass.

We got nothing done, nothing at all, and when she grew sleepy and exhausted and switched from coffee to martinis, I could stand no more. Her eyes were barely open when I stood over her and took her hand.

"Goodbye, Velda. We'll try again tomorrow." I left.

Next day everything was exactly the same except that the characters were changed, and so was the location. We sat in the gazebo out on the lawn, under the pepper tree. This time there was no coffee either, but there was a pitcher of martinis, and the sonorous, slumberous voice of Velda talking of Jean Arthur, Gary Cooper, Tyrone Power, Errol Flynn, Lily Damita, Lupe Velez, Dolores del Rio, Merle Oberon, Claude Rains, Leslie Howard, Basil Rathbone,

Nigel Bruce, Cesar Romero, George Arliss, Henry Armetta, Gregory La Cava, Paulette Goddard, Walter Wanger, Norma Talmadge, Constance Talmadge, Janet Gaynor, Frederic March, Nils Asther, Norman Foster, Ann Harding, and Kay Francis.

Chapter Fourteen

We were supposed to meet the following day, but I gagged at it. It was like suffering from a hangover, and all I saw were her wet eyes in that soft face, and all I heard was the sound of her babbling voice. I knew I could never work with her, that she would drive me crazy. I telephoned her around ten o'clock the next morning and of course the line was busy. It was busy at eleven o'clock and at noon and all that afternoon until evening. Finally I gave up and went to my typewriter and wrote her a note:

> Dear Velda:
> I must be honest with you. We will never be able to work as a team. I'm not blaming you, I blame myself. Starting tomorrow I plan to write the screenplay. When I finish I will deliver it to you, and you can edit it and improve it in any way you like. I hope this plan meets with your approval.
> > Sincerely yours,
> > Arturo Bandini

Two days later she telephoned.
"Are you sure you know what you're doing, Arturo?"
"Absolutely."
"Very well. You write the first draft and I'll follow with the final. Call me if you run into trouble."
"I will."
I began writing immediately, but the more I wrote the less I liked it. I started another draft. And another. Then a

fresh full-blown idea came to me. A new story. No more cattle men and sheep men, but something more conventional, made up of film fragments I remembered from boyhood. It moved right along. The pages piled up. It was fun. I got hot. In one sitting I wrote twenty pages.

Next day I still had a head of steam. Twenty more pages. That night I wrote until one in the morning, another fifteen pages. I loved it. I marvelled at it. How fast I was! What acuity! What dialogue! I was on to something touched with greatness. It could not fail. I saw myself a hero, an overnight sensation. And away I went: up canyons and down ravines, horse careening, six-guns blazing, Indians falling, blood in the dust, screams of women, the burning buildings, the menace of evil, the triumph of good, the victory of love. Bang bang bang a thrill a minute, the greatest goddam western story ever written. Finally, drugged on coffee, a bellyache from cigarettes, eyes burning, back aching, I finished it. Proudly I folded it into a big envelope and mailed it to Velda van der Zee. Then I took it easy and waited, knowing that there was hardly a word she could change, that she was dealing with perfection.

I spent the days on Hollywood Boulevard, in Stanley Rose's bookshop, in the off-boulevard saloons, playing the pinball games, going to movies. Then I could wait no longer, and I phoned Velda van der Zee. The line was busy. An hour later it was busy again. All day it was busy. Far into the night it was busy. In the morning I could not bear it any longer. I got into my Plymouth and shot up Benedict Canyon. The engine pinged. It needed a ring job. I pulled into Velda's driveway and knocked on the door. It was twelve o'clock. The maid greeted me.

"I came to see Velda."

"You can't," she said. "She's still asleep."

"I'll wait."

She watched me return to the car and sit behind the wheel. I was there at one o'clock, at two o'clock, at three o'clock, and at four I drove away. I drove as far as the hotel on Sunset. I went to the pay phone in the lobby, and dialled Velda's number. Even as I stood there I knew it would happen, and I was right. The line was busy. I was shaking when I stumbled toward home. I walked two blocks before I realized that I was not in my car.

The best thing about my collaboration with Velda was the money. After fifteen weeks, a three-hundred-dollar check each week, she telephoned. She had finished the script. She was sending it special delivery. It should arrive the next day. She was very proud of her work. She knew I would like it, that we had achieved a masterpiece.

"Did you change it much?" I asked.

"Here and there. Small changes. But the essence of your version, the main thrust, is still there."

"I'm glad, Velda. Frankly, I was worried."

"You're going to be very pleased, Arturo. There was so little for me to do. I hardly deserve any credit at all."

Next day I sat on the porch of Edgington's house and waited for the mailman. At noon a postal truck drove up and the driver put the large envelope in my hands. I signed the receipt, sat on the porch step, and opened the manuscript.

The title page read *Sin City*, screenplay by Velda van der Zee and Arturo Bandini, from a story by Harry Browne. I was down the first page halfway when my hair began to stiffen. In the middle of the second page I was forced to put the script aside and hang on to the porch banister. My breathing was uneven and there were mysterious shooting pains in my legs and across my stomach. I staggered to my feet and went inside to the kitchen and drank a glass of water. Edgington was sitting at the table eating breakfast. He saw my face and stood up.

"Good God, what's wrong?"

I could not speak. I could only point in the direction of the manuscript. Edgington walked to the front door and looked around.

"What's up?" he said. "Who's out there?"

I came through the house to the porch and pointed at the manuscript. He picked it up.

"What's this?" He looked at the title page. "What's wrong with it?"

"Read it."

He took it to the porch swing and sat down.

"I've been had," I said. "I didn't write it. My name's on it, but I didn't write it."

He began to read. Suddenly he laughed, a short barking laugh. "It's funny," he said. "It's a very funny script."

"You mean it's a comedy?"

"That's what's funny. It's not a comedy." He went back to the script and read in silence, another ten pages. Then, deliberately, he folded the manuscript shut and looked at me.

"Is it still funny?"

He rolled up the script and threw it into an ivy patch beyond the porch.

"It's ghastly," he said.

I rescued the script from the ivy bed. He had read my version more than fifteen weeks ago. He had liked it, praised it.

"What should I do?" I asked.

"How about going back to Colorado and learning to lay brick with your old man?"

"That's no solution."

"The only solution is to get your name off this script. Disown it. Don't be associated with it."

"Maybe I can save it."

"Save it from what? It's dead, man. It's been murdered. Call your agent and tell him to remove your name. Either that or get out of town." He rose and walked back into the kitchen. I opened the screenplay and started to read again. What I read was as follows:

A stagecoach rolls across the Wyoming plain pursued by band of Indians. Stagecoach brought to halt. Indians swarm over it. Two passengers: Reverend Ezra Drew and daughter Priscilla. Indian chief drags Priscilla out, throws her on his horse. Priscilla struggles. Chief mounts, rides off with her. Indians follow.

Indian village. Chief rides up with Priscilla, shoves her into teepee, then enters. Indian chief is Magua, enemy of white man. He seizes girl, handles her roughly, kissing her as she struggles.

Over the hill comes posse, led by Sheriff Lawson. He dismounts, hears girl scream, enters teepee, struggles with Magua, knocks him down, helps girl outside, puts her in saddle of his horse, mounts, and rides off. Posse follows.

Sin City. Posse arrives, Sheriff puts Priscilla down. Posse brings up Reverend Drew. Priscilla runs into his arms. Townspeople gather. Sheriff Lawson leads Priscilla into Sin City Hotel.

That night townfolk gather at hotel. Sheriff comes out with Priscilla and Reverend Drew. Townfolk beg them to stay. Local church recently burned out by hostile Indians of Chief Magua. People urge Reverend Drew to rebuild church. He promises to consider it. Playing banjo, Reverend Drew accompanies daughter in singing of "I Love You, Jesus." Great applause. Holding tambourine, Priscilla moves among townfolk and they drop coins into tambourine. Reverend Drew mounts hotel porch and delivers speech. He and daughter promise to remain and rebuild Sin City church. Citizens repair to big saloon. Once more the Reverend strums banjo and Priscilla sings "Lord Welcome Me." Again she passes tambourine and makes generous collection.

Church being rebuilt. Townspeople help, carrying lumber and building material. Sheriff rides up and puts Priscilla in his buckboard. They ride off. In lovely pine grove Sheriff embraces Priscilla and they kiss.

Evening. Sin City saloon. Priscilla sings "The Lord Is My Shepherd," while saloon patrons listen and admire the lovely young woman. She passes tambourine. A drunk at bar seizes her, tries to kiss her. Sheriff Lawson intervenes, fight develops. Lawson knocks intruder down. Priscilla looks to Sheriff gratefully.

On hillside overlooking town sits the sinister Magua on his horse, watching. He dismounts and slinks to window of saloon as Priscilla addresses bar patrons in little speech. She wants townsfolk to form a church choir where hymns can be sung and offerings made for new church. Townspeople agree and applaud. Outside at window the evil Magua smirks as he listens.

Change comes over Sin City. No more liquor in town saloon. No more gambling. Group of women under Priscilla's direction sing spirited hymns. Work on church proceeds. Day arrives when church is complete, and townfolk gather for first service. Watching from above, Magua observes the happenings below and rides off.

Evening. Women of Sin City prepare barbecue outside church. A square dance in progress, led by Reverend Drew and his banjo. Priscilla whirls to music, her partner the Sheriff. Meanwhile at Indian village Magua gathers his forces. Indians with painted bodies mount their horses and Magua leads them away.

Square dance. Sheriff leads Priscilla into woods. She lifts face for his kiss. He asks her to marry him. She consents. Suddenly the sound of pounding hoofs and Indian yells. Down the hill come Magua and his bloodthirsty Arapahoes. Riding furiously, they ring the church and townspeople with bloodcurdling shouts and thundering hoofs. Shrieking townfolk retreat to church as Indians continue to circle and fire their rifles. Sheriff and Priscilla rush to safety of new church. Round and round the Indians tighten their noose about the church. Gunfire. Cries of wounded. Indians hurl torches upon church roof. Townsfolk mount gun positions at church windows. Battle rages. Women reload rifles. Priscilla reloads her father's rifle. At that moment he is shot. Priscilla shoots Indian who felled her father. Then she turns and gathers fallen parent in her arms and cries.

Meanwhile the treacherous Magua has dismounted and

comes slithering toward church door. He enters unseen and swoops down on Priscilla, cups hand over her mouth, and drags her outside. Throwing her upon back of his horse, he mounts behind her and rides off just as Sheriff Lawson appears in doorway. Taking dead aim, Magua fires rifle at Sheriff and bullet strikes him in shoulder. Lawson staggers but does not go down. Instead he lurches toward Magua, who rides off with the struggling Priscilla.

Wounded but undaunted, Sheriff gropes to his horse, mounts, and rides in pursuit. Over hill and dale he follows fleeing Indian and girl. They come to a creek in the foothills and stop. Bleeding and weak, Lawson rides up, then falls to the ground. Eagerly Magua dismounts with menacing tomahawk. Fierce battle, men rolling and twisting, Priscilla watching in horror. They fall into creek. Magua leaps upon weakened Sheriff and tries to drown him, but Sheriff frees himself.

Too weak to resist further, Sheriff collapses in water. With yell of triumph Magua raises tomahawk to strike. Suddenly the crack of a rifle breaks the stillness. Magua falls into the water. Priscilla, smoking rifle in her hands, dismounts and rushes to Sheriff. She drags him from creek. Weakened but defiant, Sheriff throws arms around her. They rise and stagger away. In the water Magua lies dead.

Back in Sin City church siege goes on. Whites slowly gain upper hand. Launch counter attack. Hand to hand combat. Many Indians retreat. Others captured by townsfolk. A dozen savages being led to city jail. In the distance come Priscilla and Sheriff Lawson. Strapped across their horse is body of dead Magua. Great cheer from townsfolk. Priscilla runs into father's arms.

Epilogue. Bright Sunday morning. Songfest comes from church. Inside Priscilla leads choir in "Oh Gentle Jesus." Church packed with townsfolk listening reverently. In back pews, segregated from others, are a dozen captive Indians, penitent, heads bowed. Sheriff comes to Priscilla's side. She looks up adoringly. Fade out.

So there it was, the whole dirty business. My screenplay, without a line of my work in it, in fact an altogether different story, impossible for me to have concocted. I laughed. It was a joke. Somebody was playing around. It was impossible. I went into the house and sat there smoking cigarettes, suddenly aware of the falling rain, the sweet sound of it on the shingle roof, the sweet smell of it coming through the front door. No question about it, Edgington was right. My only course was to have my name removed from the title. I picked up the telephone and dialled Cyril Korn.

"Yeah?" he barked.

"Hello, Korn. This is me. Have you read the story?"

"I liked it."

"You're crazy."

"It's a great western."

"Take my name off."

"What?"

"Remove my name from this monstrosity. You hear me? I want no part of it."

There was a long silence before Korn spoke again. Then he said:

"Suit yourself, kid. This is good news for Velda. She'll get a solo credit now."

"She can have it." I hung up.

The rain came down in sheets, whipping the leaves from the eucalyptus trees, digging little rivers across the yard and into the gutter. I drank a glass of wine. Edgington stepped out of the kitchen. He had heard my conversation with Korn.

"You did right," he said. "It was self preservation. You had no choice. If you'd listened to me this wouldn't have happened."

"What do you mean?"

"You should have joined the Guild. I've been telling you for three months."

The cold rainy wind swept in through the front door, chilling the room. Edgington went to the fireplace and lit the gas logs. He took a tobacco sack from his pocket.

"Here," he said, tossing it to me.

It was marijuana. There were cigarette papers in the sack. I had smoked marijuana only once before, in Boulder, and it made me sick. It was time to get sick again. I rolled a cigarette. We sat looking at one another, drawing down the weed into our lungs. Edgington laughed. I laughed too.

"You're a rotten no-good sonofabitchin English limey toad," I said.

He nodded agreement. "And you, sir, are a miserable, disagreeable dago dog."

We lapsed into silence, smoking the grass. I picked up the manuscript.

"Let's do something to it," I said.

"Let's burn it."

I took it to the fireplace and dropped it on the flames. The pot was taking over. I took off my shirt.

"Let's be Indians," I said. "Let's burn her at the stake."

"Great," Edington said, pulling off his shirt.

"Let's take off our pants," I said. We laughed and kicked off our pants. In a moment we were naked, dancing in a circle, making what we thought were Indian cries. From the clouds came a clap of thunder. We laughed and rolled on the floor. Edgington had a beer. I drank a glass of wine. The downpour was earshattering. I rushed out and we held hands and danced round and round laughing. I ran into the house, sipped on my wine and ran outside again. Edgington rushed in, took a swig of his beer, and joined me in the rain. We lay on the grass, rolling in the rain, shouting at the thunder. A woman's voice pierced the storm. It was from next door.

"Shame on you, Frank Edgington," she screamed. "Put on some clothes before I call the police."

Frank got to his feet and shoved his bare bottom toward her

"That for you, Martha!"

We ran into the house. Standing before the fireplace, dripping wet, we watched the sparks from Velda's screenplay dancing up the chimney. We looked at one another and smiled. Then we performed a fitting climax to the whole crazy ritual. We pissed on the fire.

Now a curious thing happened. I looked at Edgington's sopping hair and rain-soaked body and I did not like him. I did not like him at all. There was something obscene about our nakedness, and the burning screenplay, and the floor wet from rain, and our bodies shivering in the cold, and the insolent smile from Edgington's lips, and I recoiled from him, and blamed him for everything. After all, hadn't he sent me to Cyril Korn, and hadn't Cyril Korn brought me together with Velda van der Zee, and hadn't Edgington sneered and scoffed all the weeks that I had been writing the screenplay? I no longer liked this man. He disgusted me. Similar thoughts must have boiled up in his brain for I noticed the hostile sharpness of his glance. We did not speak. We stood there hating one another. We were on the verge of fighting. I picked up my clothes, walked into the bedroom and slammed the door.

Chapter Fifteen

After that it was a feud. When he was at work in the studio I loafed about, drinking wine and playing the radio. Day after day the rain beat down. I sat at my desk in the bedroom and tried to write. Nothing came. It was the house, Edgington's house. I had to get away from him. Whenever he returned from the studio I pretended to be busy at the desk pecking at the typewriter. He stayed only a short while, then he was gone again. One day I found an old *New Yorker* in a stack of magazines. It contained a story Edgington had written. I tore it up. I began going out, getting into my car and driving off in the rain. The storm was exasperating. The streets were like rivers. Manhole covers popped from storm drains. Trees fell. Wilshire was a barricade of sandbags. The streets were deserted. I drove into Hollywood and sat in a saloon on Wilcox, drinking wine and playing the pinball games. Sometimes I parked at Musso-Frank's and sloshed through the rain to the restaurant. I knew no one. I ate alone and felt my hatred for the town. I went next door to Stanley Rose's bookshop. Nobody knew me. I hung around like a bird seeking crumbs. I missed Mrs. Brownell and Abe Marx and Du Mont. My memory of Jennifer Lovelace almost broke my heart. Knowing those few had made me feel as if I knew thousands in the city. I drove to Bunker Hill and parked in front of the hotel, but I could not bring myself to go inside. Suddenly I had a dream, a beautiful dream of a novel. It was about Helen Brownell and myself. I could taste it. I could embrace it. All at once the self pity drained from me. There was life still, there was a typewriter and paper and eyes to see them, and thoughts to keep them alive. I sat in my car at the top of Bunker Hill in the rain and the dream enfolded me, and I knew what I would do. I would go to Terminal Island and find myself a fisherman's shack on the sandy beach and sit there and write a novel about Helen Brownell and myself. I would spend months in that shack, piling up the pages while I smoked a Meerschaum pipe and became a writer once more in the world.

I hoped to pack my stuff and get out of there before Edgington returned, but as I drove up to his bungalow I saw his car in the driveway. I got out and ran through the rain to the house. Frank lay on the couch reading a book. He said "Hi." I walked past him into my room and began to pack. After a while he arose and stood in the bedroom door with a magazine in his hand.

"I bring you good tidings of great joy," he smiled, holding out the magazine. It was a copy of *Daily Variety*. I spread it open and saw red pencil markings around a front page story. It read:

> Velda van der Zee, who screenplayed *Sin City* for Liberty Films, will also direct opus, according to producer Jack Arthur. Film casting will terminate this week and shooting will commence in Arizona.

I was in shock, but hid it from Edgington, and tossed him the magazine. "This makes you very happy, doesn't it?" I said. He smiled and shrugged.

"C'est la vie."

I went back to my packing, filled a suitcase and carried it out to the car, where the rest of my things—typewriter, books, clothing—were piled up in the back seat. Now that I was ready to leave for the last time there was one matter not concluded. I stood beside the car and gathered resolve. I would probably never encounter Edgington again. How could I impress upon him the memory of this departure on this rainy day? At last I resolved the matter and walked back to the house. He was on the couch.

"I'm leaving now," I said.

He stood up and offered his hand. "Good luck, dago."

I hit him in the face and knocked him down on the couch. He sat there nursing a nosebleed. I walked back to the car and drove away. I shouldn't have struck Edgington. He had been hospitable and friendly and generous and kind. But I couldn't bear his arrogance. He was too successful for me. He had it coming. I had no regrets. That was life. I was sorry for his nosebleed, but he deserved it. As for Velda van der Zee, fuck her. What was another director? The town was crawling with them.

Chapter Sixteen

I drove to Avalon Boulevard and south to Wilmington. It was almost sunset as I passed over the bridge onto the big sandbar known as Terminal Island. The rain had washed the sand from the road and I drove on pavement to the little fishing settlement a mile or so from the canneries. There were six rustic bungalows, all in a row facing the channel waters a hundred yards down the beach. None of the bungalows appeared to be occupied. I drove slowly past them. Each showed a "For Rent" sign on the front porch. Then I noticed a light in the last house. Exactly like the others, the house was dark green and rainsoaked. The light shone through the open front door. I pulled to a stop and ran through the rain to the porch.

In ten minutes I had rented one of the cottages and moved in. It was the center cottage, combination bedroom, living room, and a kitchen and bath. Twenty-five dollars a month. I did some quick calculations and realized that I had enough money to live there for ten years. I had it made.

The place was paradise, the South Pacific, Bora Bora. I could hear the sea. It came whispering, saying shshsh, for it was always low tide, the island protected by a breakwater. The nights were wondrous. I lay on my small cot and felt the memory of Velda van der Zee slipping from me. In a few days it had vanished. I listened to the sea and felt my heart restored. Sometimes I heard the bark of seals. I stood in the door and watched them in the shallow water, three or four big fellows playing in the soft tide, barking as if to laugh.

The city was far away. I had no thought of writing. My mind was barren as the long shore. I was Robinson Crusoe, lost in a distant world, at peace, breathing good air, salty, satisfying.

When day broke I walked barefoot in the water, in the moist sand, a mile to the cannery settlement, teeming with workers, men and women, emptying the fishing boats, dressing and canning the fish in big corrugated buildings. They were mostly Japanese and Mexican folk from San Pedro. There were two restaurants. The food was good and cheap. Sometimes I walked to the end of the pier, to the ferryboat landing, where the boats took off across the channel to San Pedro. It was twenty-five cents round trip. I felt like a millionaire whenever I plunked down my quarter and sailed for Pedro. I rented a bike and toured the Palos Verdes hills. I found the public library and loaded up on books. Back at my shack I built a fire in the woodstove and sat in the warmth and read Dostoevsky and Flaubert and Dickens and all those famous people. I lacked for nothing. My life was a prayer, a thanksgiving. My loneliness was an enrichment. I found myself bearable, tolerable, even good. Sometimes I wondered what had happened to the writer who had come there. Had I written something and left the place? I touched my typewriter and mused at the action of the keys. It was another life. I had never been here before. I would never leave it.

My landlady was a Japanese woman. She was pregnant. She had a noble kind of walk, small steps, very quiet, her black hair in braids. I learned from her how to bow. We were always bowing. Sometimes we walked on the beach too. We stopped, folded our hands and bowed. Then she went her way and I went mine. One day I found a rowboat flopping along the shore. I got in and rowed away, doing poorly, for I could not manage the oars. But I learned how, and pulled the skiff all the way across the channel to the rocks on the San Pedro side. I bought fishing equipment and bait, and rowed out a hundred yards beyond my house and caught corbina and mackerel, and once a halibut. I brought them home and cooked them and they were ghastly, and I threw them out upon the sand, and watchful seagulls swooped down and carried them away. One day I said, I must write something. I wrote a letter to my mother, but I could not date the letter. I had no memory of time. I went to see the Japanese lady and asked her the date of the month.

"January fourth," she said.

I smiled. I had been there two months, and thought it no more than two weeks.

Chapter Seventeen

One afternoon as I dozed, I heard a car outside. I went to the door and watched a long red Marmon touring car pull up to the house next door. The car had a royal insignia painted on the hood—a crown with crouching lions in red and gold. Beneath was the inscription: Duke of Sardinia. The driver of the car shut off the engine and stepped down. He was short and powerful, his black hair in a crew cut. He was so muscular he seemed made of rubber, his arms like red sewer pipe, his legs so thick a space separated them. He saw me and smiled.

"How you say?" he asked.

"Fine, fine. How you?"

"Purty good. You live here?"

"Yep."

"We neighbors." He crossed to me and shook my hand. I nodded at his Marmon.

"Duke of Sardinia, what's that mean?"

"I am son of the prince of Sardinia. Also champion of the world."

"You a weight lifter?"

"Rassler. World champion. I come here to train."

He moved to the wagon hitched to the back of the car. It was a two-wheeled vehicle with enormous spokes, a big cart. The bed of the vehicle was piled with gym mats, weight-lifting paraphernalia, and sports equipment. He began unloading the cart.

"Who you?" he asked.

I told him.

"Italiano?"

"Sure."

He smiled. "That's good."

I watched him unload the cart for a while. Then I went inside. It had been weeks since I sat down before the typewriter. I began a letter to my mother. After a while I felt a pair of intense eyes drilling the back of my neck. I turned. The Duke stood in the doorway watching me.

"Come in," I said.

He entered and carefully inspected the room, the walls, the sink, and finally the typewriter.

"Write some more," he said, gesturing. "Don't stop." He sat across from me and I pecked away at the letter.

"What you write?" he asked.

"Stories. Movies. Sometimes poetry."

"You make money?"

I laughed. "Naturally. Big money."

He grinned doubtfully and stood up. "I go now. Time to work out."

Half an hour later I heard the cluck and clatter of cartwheels as the Duke of Sardinia pulled the empty cart out upon the beach. He was in wrestler's tights and barefooted, hitched to the tongue of the cart by a strap about his waist and another strap from his forehead down to the front of the cart. He pulled the cart without effort, the big wheels crunching in the soft sand. After he had gone a few yards he snatched a shovel from the cart and began filling the vehicle with sand. I walked out and watched him. Sweat was popping from his back and down his neck. He worked furiously.

"What are you doing?" I asked.

"Workout," he panted, continuing to shovel. It wasn't long before the cart was full. He threw the shovel atop the load, adjusted the harness around his waist, fixed the strap about his forehead, grunted mightily and began to pull. The wheels dug into the sand, but there was no progress. He struggled, his feet gave way, he fell, he struggled and tried again. I pitied him. I leaped to help him, butting my shoulder against the back of the cart. It began to move. The Duke turned in shock and saw me. Enraged, he grabbed me under the armpits and threw me across the sand. I landed on my back with a thud that took my breath away.

"No," he said, shaking his fist. "Go away. I train myself."

I sat there gasping, watching him get into his harness and try again. The Duke of Sardinia! He had to be crazy. I turned my back and went into the house. An hour later I stepped out on the porch and saw him far down the beach. He seemed barely to move, like a distant turtle. It was two hours before he pulled the cart up to his house. His body was awash with sweat. Sand clung to the sweat, and he looked frosted, and very tired. I watched him trot to the edge of the water, then fling himself into the depths. He played in the water like a short, stumpy fish. It was dark when he dragged himself out and came back to his porch. I watched him towel off.

"You like spaghett'?" he asked.

"Yeah."

"I fix."

Next day he heard my typewriter and came inside again. He sat there watching me rattle the keys.

"What you write now?"

"Letter."

"You write poetry?"

"Any time."

"How much for one poetry?"

I looked at him. I really didn't like him very much. He had handled me badly the day before. And there was this insolent smile, and his preposterous title. He was stupid and I would use it against him.

"Ten dollars," I said. "Ten dollars for ten lines. What do you want me to write about?"

"I have woman in Lompoc. She like poetry."

"Love?" I said.

"Yeah."

I turned to the typewriter, wrenched myself into a poetic mood, and began to peck away:

O paramour of New Hebrides
Beseech me not to deride thy trust.
Love's a strophe amid the bloom of lost heavens.
Bring me the weal and woe of scattered dreams.
My heart lusts for fin de siècle,
That vision of beleaguered days.
Want not, oh love! Look to the bastions!
Flee the scoundrel, grant mercy only to love,
And when the bounty is sated in reparation
Believe what is in my heart.

I cleared my throat and read it to the Duke.

"She'sa beautiful," he said. "I take. Give me pencil."

I handed him a pencil. He spread out the page of poetry and signed it below the bottom line. It read: "Mario, Duke of Sardinia."

"You have envelope?" he asked.

I took one from the desk and rolled it into the typewriter. "Send to Jenny Palladino, 121 Celery Avenue, Lompoc."

I typed it out and he went away.

At supper time he returned with a tureen of cooked white spaghetti. I rolled a forkful of the pasta and put it in my mouth. It was terrifying—a sauce of garlic, onions, and hot peppers. It simply would not go down. I leaped for a bottle of wine. The Duke laughed.

"Make you strong," he said, "be a man."

But I couldn't eat it. He took the plate from me and ate methodically, down to the last white strand. I poured us glasses of wine, and lit a cigarette.

"How about some more poetry?"

He shrugged. "One more—maybe."

I turned to my typewriter and wrote effortlessly, ten lines. The Duke watched with folded arms.

"Want to hear it?" I asked.

"Sure—I listen."

I read:

> O tumbrels in the night past the lugubrious sea,
> Mute birds ride thy salt-soaked wheels.
> Heaviness brings the clouds down to earth,
> Seeking the tracks of the wheels.
> Gulls cry, fish leap, the moon appears.
> Where are the children?
> What happened to the children?
> My love is away, and the children are gone.
> A dark boat passes on the horizon.
> What has happened here?

The Duke lifted the poem from my hand and curled his lip dubiously.

"You don't like it?" I asked.

"I give you seven dollars."

I snatched the poem from his hand. "No deal. It's a good poem. One of my best. Don't chisel me. If you don't like it, say so."

He sighed. "Putum in the mailbox." He meant the envelope.

He dug a roll of bills from his pocket and peeled off a ten spot. I thanked him for it and put it away. Turning to the typewriter I said:

"Now I'm going to give you a little bonus, Duke. Something you'll really appreciate." I began to type out my favorite sonnet from Rupert Brooke, *The Hill:*

> Breathless, we flung us on the windy hill,
> Laughed in the sun, and kissed the lovely grass.
> You said, "Through glory and ecstasy we pass;
> Wind, sun, and earth remain, the birds sing still,
> When we are old, are old. . . ." "And when we die
> All's over that is ours; and life burns on
> Through other lovers, other lips," said I,
> "Heart of my heart, our heaven is now, is won!"
> "We are Earth's best, that learnt her lesson here.

Life is our cry. We have kept the faith!" we said;
"We shall go down with unreluctant tread
Rose-crowned into the darkness! . . ." Proud we were,
And laughed, that had such brave true things to say.
And then you suddenly cried, and turned away.

As I finished reading it, his mouth was curled in annoyance, and he snatched the paper from my hand, studying it, glaring at it, half crumpled in his fist.

"Steenk!" he exclaimed, crushing the page into a ball, and throwing it on the floor. He was a very short man, but as he got to his feet he took on the enormity of a great turtle. Suddenly his hands were under my armpits and I was lifted toward the ceiling, and shaken violently. His livid face and smoldering dark eyes looked up at me.

"Nobody cheat Duke of Sardinia. *Capeesh?*" His fingers opened and I dropped heavily into my chair. As he left, the crushed ball of paper lay in his way. He gave it a violent kick and walked out.

Chapter Eighteen

Every day the Duke pulled his wagon of sand a mile up the beach to the cannery and back. One afternoon I timed him. It took two hours. He always returned in the same state of exhaustion, falling flat on his face in the sand. I wanted to be friends. I smiled, said "Hi," but he was still offended, until one afternoon, sweat pouring from him, he said:

"Tomorrow I fight. Olympic Auditorium. You come." I was startled, about to say something, but he grabbed my jaw. "Tomorrow! Understand?"

I shook my head. "Who you fighting, Duke?"

"Animal," he said. "Name of Richard Lionheart."

"Is he good?"

"He'sa good. I kill him anyway."

He trudged toward the water and dove in, happy as a porpoise. I had no desire to go to his wrestling match. The more I thought of it the more I resented him, but there was a simple way out of the matter. I would get into my car and drive into Wilmington and go to a movie. He came dripping out of the water and towelled himself on the porch.

"We take my car tomorrow," he said. "Leave six o'clock. Be ready." He went into his house.

I didn't want any part of his goddamned fight, and I resolved not to go. All that day I sat about nurturing my resolve not to go with him, and by bedtime I had worked myself into such a frenzied protest that sleep was impossible. All night I rolled and tossed. At two in the morning I could stand it no more, and I got up and dressed quietly. On tiptoe I walked to the door and went outside, careful not to produce a loud squeal in the screendoor. Quietly I crossed to my car and slipped behind the wheel. As I turned the starter key a hand clutched me by the throat. There stood the Duke.

"Where you go?" he asked.

"To get a candy bar," I improvised.

"Too late for candy bar," he said. "Go to bed."

I got out of the car and walked back to the house. He followed me like a tireless cop. I slammed the front door and locked it. I was so mad I wanted to kill him. I threw open the front door and yelled at him:

"Fuck you, you no good peasant wop! I hate your guts! I'm not coming to your fight tomorrow—not even to see your head knocked off! You're scum! You're a fake and a farce and a scum! You know how dumb you are? You're so dumb you didn't even like a Rupert Brooke poem. I fooled you, you ignoramus. Pure Brooke, and you didn't like it!"

I slammed the door, locked it, and went to bed.

Next morning I found him sitting on my front porch. He stared at me with contrite eyes.

"You mad?" he asked.

"No."

"You are my friend. I like you."

"I like you too."

"I go alone to fight."

"Is it so important?"

"The fans don't like me. I need someone in my corner."

I sighed. "Okay, Duke. I'll go with you."

He crossed to me and put his hand over the back of my neck and shook me gently. *"Grazie,"* he smiled.

The papers said the wrestling matches that Thursday night attracted five thousand people. The Duke of Sardinia was right—everyone in the place with the exception of myself hated him. From the moment we got out of his car in the parking lot and walked toward the Olympic Auditorium, he gathered an increasingly hostile crowd. They were Mexicans, blacks, and gringos, heckling him, throwing things at him, calling him obscene names. I walked beside him and felt the breaking waves of hate.

As we entered a side door reserved for fighters, a huge black man loomed before us and flung a lemon pie in the Duke's face. It did not shame the Duke at all. Instead he charged like a terrier, throwing a scissors hold around the black man's legs, and toppling him. Then the Duke sat on him and smeared the lemon pie from his own face to that of the black man. Instantly a crowd boiled up, tearing the two men apart. The police arrived, and whisked the Duke down the hall to the dressing room. The Duke was invigorated now, full of fight, ready for Richard Lionheart.

At fight time I followed my gladiator into the arena and down the aisle to the ring. The hatred he generated entered my bones. I could not understand why the crowd disliked him so. Still, he need not have sneered so blatantly, or gestured back so obscenely. A woman leaped from her seat and slapped him in the face. The Duke sneered and spat at her. Several ushers gathered below ringside and protected him as he climbed into the ring. He walked about, shaking his fist, the crowd shrieked in rage, and again the onslaught of debris flung at him. The referee entered the ring and asked him to sit down. The Duke did so, and the scene quieted.

After a moment or two a roar of approval rose from the throats of the crowd. There were whistles and cheers as Richard Lionheart appeared. He was garbed in a white silk robe. His shoes were a soft blue, and his lovely blond hair, carefully coiffured, hung down to his shoulders. He was beautiful, and the crowd adored him. He removed his white robe and revealed powder blue trunks. He bowed grandly to one and all. Then, quite ostentatiously, he knelt in the center of the ring, made the sign of the cross, bowed his head, closed his eyes, and prayed. Suddenly the Duke leaped from his corner and kicked out with both feet, knocking Richard flat on the canvas. The crowd was like a pack of lions. Things were hurled—things like chairs and bottles, fruit and tomatoes, and now I knew why everybody hated this man. He was the enemy.

The drama was clear. The Duke could not win in this ring. He would dish out a lot of punishment, for he was the devil, but Richard Lionheart, blessed with purity, would conquer him in the end. It was what the crowd came to see and paid its money for.

Chapter Nineteen

The fight began with the two wrestlers facing one another in the center of the ring. The Duke was five feet two and weighed 235. Richard Lionheart was six feet eight and weighed 235. They moved about, sparring for a grip. Quickly, the Duke slipped between Lionheart's legs and grasped the big man's flowing coiffure. He went down like a ton of coal. The Duke leaped upon him, and managed a scissor hold around his neck. Lionheart kicked helplessly, his face turning blue. The crowd was on its feet, shrieking in rage. A woman climbed through the ropes and smacked the Duke in the face several times with her purse. The crowd cheered. Two other women scrambled into the ring, removed their shoes, and delivered a terrible pasting to the rugged Italiano, forcing him to break his scissor hold on Lionheart's neck.

The referee cleared the ring and the two wrestlers confronted one another again. This time Lionheart got the advantage, hoisting the Duke above his head and whirling him round and round, then hurling him violently to the canvas. The crowd shrieked with joy. The Duke lay still, seemingly unconscious. Lionheart picked him up, carried him to the edge of the ring and dropped him over the ropes and into the laps of three women. He seemed senseless, motionless. The women dumped him on the floor and stomped him. He rolled away from them, staggered to his feet, and climbed painfully back into the ring, his face covered with blood.

The referee blew his whistle and helped the Duke into his

corner. A doctor was called. He wiped the blood away, pronounced the Duke in good shape, and ordered the fight to continue. The Duke lumbered to his feet, but so stunned was he that he wandered about the ring in a daze. From across the ring Lionheart took dead aim and butted the Duke in the stomach. Down went the Duke again. Lionheart hurled himself on the prone body, seized the Duke's foot and bent it backward in a frightening toehold. The crowd, fascinated, seemed to croon with pleasure. The referee bent down to determine if the Duke's shoulders had touched the canvas. The triumphant Lionheart, still bending the Duke's foot deep into the small of his back, waved at the crowd, and the crowd waved back. I was not worried about the Duke's defeat so much as his death, for he was motionless, eyes closed, panting heavily.

Suddenly he made his move, and his short thick arms thrust out toward Lionheart's flowing locks. Horror transfixed the crowd. A roar of agony filled the auditorium, as the Duke's hands formed two fistfuls of golden hair, and flung Lionheart aside. Grotesquely, like a crab righting himself, the Duke clung to the hair as he struggled to his feet. Women shrieked. Some wept as he pulled Lionheart about the ring by the hair.

He varied his attack. Now he kicked Lionheart in the jaw. Now he sat on his face and bounced his body mercilessly, laughing at the crowd, jeering at their protests. Then he had Lionheart on his back, his shoulders perilously close to the canvas. Suddenly the beautiful man collapsed, his shoulders touching. The Duke sat on him and tweaked his nose. It was an unbearable insult. The referee pronounced the Duke winner of the first fall.

The crowd could not bear it. All five thousand crowded the ring and a dozen fans descended on the Duke of Sardinia. They would have rent his body to shreds had not the police intervened. He was escorted from the ring and down the aisle to his dressing room.

Lionheart's handlers lifted him to his stool in the corner. His right leg stood out stiffly. A doctor entered the ring and examined him. Lionheart was in tears. The doctor and the referee spoke together quietly. A judge at ringside rang the bell. In the quiet that followed the referee declared the fight a draw, and since Lionheart could not continue, the match was terminated. Bedlam followed. Lionheart's followers poured into the ring and attacked the referee, tearing off his shirt and beating him to the canvas. Police leaped to his rescue as I scurried down the aisle to the rear of the auditorium.

The Duke lay on a rubbing table in his dressing room, a trainer massaging his muscles. He smiled as I walked over.

"Purty good, no?" he asked.

"It was a draw, Duke."

"Draw?" He leaped off the rubbing table. "Who say so?"

"The referee."

The Duke shot out of the dressing room and down the hall. I watched him fight his way through a crowd thronging the aisle. The police were on him instantly, carrying him struggling and screaming back to the dressing room, and shutting the door behind him. I stood in the hall for ten minutes, wondering what to do. Inside the dressing room the Duke screamed and threw furniture.

I walked back to the arena and watched two wrestlers grappling in the ring. It bored me. I walked out to the car and lit a cigarette. For an hour I awaited the Duke's appearance. The final match ended and the crowd poured out to the parking lot. One by one the cars drove away until only the Duke's Marmon remained.

It was an hour later, at midnight, when he strode to the car. He got in beside me and I saw that his face was badly cut, his nose bleeding, his knuckles and his trousers splattered with blood. He reached into the glove compartment and took out a packet of paper towels. He dabbed his broken and bleeding face. I saw a water hydrant at the corner of the building, and told him. He stepped from the car and walked to the hydrant and turned it on. He rubbed his hands into the flowing water, then cupping them he flushed his face. I felt sorrow for him. Someone had beaten him up, and he was angry and stoical and brooding. We went back to the car and got in. I held the roll of paper towels. Every now and then he held out his hand and I gave him a fresh batch of towels. We drove to Avalon and turned right toward the harbor. He drove in silence except that now and then he sobbed.

Chapter Twenty

All the next day the Duke lay in bed, his face to the wall. Whenever I knocked on the door and entered he did not move.

"Are you okay?" I asked.

"Thank you. Go away."

The next day it was the same. I could not detect any movement in his body at all.

"Can I get you anything?"

"No. Go away."

"You have to eat something, Duke."

"Please. Leave me alone."

The morning of the third day I was asleep when I heard his Marmon revving up outside. I went to the door and watched him back the car out. He saw me and pressed the brakes. I went down to the car. He looked refreshed and smiling.

"Feeling okay?"

"Feeling good. I go to Los Angeles for a fight."

"Who you fighting?"

"I fight Lionheart again. I go for rematch. This time I kill him." He shifted gears, waved, and drove off. He was gone all day and far into the night. Around midnight I heard him drive in.

In the morning I heard the big cart being moved, the wheels clucking in the sand. The Duke was back in business. I watched him harness his body to the wagon and push off in the soft white sand. I went out on the porch and called out:

"When do you fight?"

"Two weeks. Olympic Auditorium."

"It's bad, Duke. The fans hate you over there."

He grinned.

"No, no. They love me. Everybody love the Duke of Sardinia."

I was sitting on the porch reading Melville when the car drove up. It was a model-A Ford, and the driver was a girl. She shut the engine and stepped out. I looked up the beach. The Duke was not in sight. The girl crossed to his front porch and knocked on the door. She was gorgeous in a blue polka dot skirt and a blue sweater. Her ass was from heaven. Her face was exquisitely refined in the frame of her dark hair and sparkling eyes.

"He's not here," I said. "He's working out on the beach."

She looked up and down the sand. "Which way did he go?"

I nodded. "He's pulling a big red cart."

"Thank you," she said. "Will he be long?"

"Maybe an hour. The Duke and I are friends. Why don't you sit down and wait?"

She glanced about for a chair.

"I'm sorry," I said. "Would you like to come inside?"

"No, thank you." She leaned against the post and lapsed into silence. I stood up. "Can I get you something? How about some coffee? I just made it."

"No thank you."

"I'm Arturo Bandini."

She smiled. "How do you do? I'm Jenny Palladino."

"From Lompoc," I smiled.

Startled, she asked, "How did you know?"

"The Duke mentioned it." I held open the screendoor. "Please come in. I make wonderful coffee."

"No thanks."

"Don't be afraid. If you're a friend of the Duke's, you're perfectly safe here. Do I look like someone who'd make a pass at the girlfriend of the Duke of Sardinia?"

Her face studied me seriously, then she smiled. "I guess not."

"Come in," I urged. "Be my guest."

"Well. . . ." she hesitated.

"Please don't worry. I'm deathly afraid of the Duke."

She entered. I led her to the best chair and she sat down. All at once a sense of frivolity overcame me. There was something disapproving in her eyes and the jut of her lower lip. I had no thought of making a pass. I merely wanted to play, to enter into some sort of game with her. I poured her a cup of coffee and she thanked me and sipped it. She was beautiful and sensuous and wonderfully formed, yet I had no desire for her, only a wish to tumble about with her in the manner of kittens. I dropped to one knee before her, and she quickly pulled her feet up on the chair.

"Oh thou loveliest of the children of Eve," I intoned, "sweet are thy eyes, and the wonderment of their arch. Bless you, lovely maiden, in the curvature of your sculptured neck. Seek not to banish me, for I long to bask in the glow of thy wondrous eyes."

Her lips turned in a frown. "So you're the one!" she said. "I knew it wasn't the Duke. It couldn't be."

I'm not going to hurt her, I said to myself. I'm not going to seduce her. I only want to make her smile.

"Listen, oh love! to the flight of the partridge, winging through the open barn, seeking his love in the fresh-mown hay. Bring her to me, oh wandering birds, suffer her not to flee in fear."

She jumped to her feet, and pushed me aside. "Leave me alone," she said. Then she screamed:

"Duke! Duke!"

She paused to remove her shoes, and then she was off like a terrified deer. In the distance, appearing now, I saw the cumbersome figure of the Duke at the helm of his red wagon. I stood there in terror for a moment. Then I did what had to be done.

I flung my clothes into the suitcases, gathered up my typewriter, and ran to my car, tossing everything into the back seat. I rushed into the house again for another load. On the way out I saw Jenny Palladino confronting the Duke, and gesticulating with both hands. He unharnessed himself and broke into a run toward me. I gathered the books and a raincoat, ran to the car, and started the engine. The Duke was fifty feet away when I shot out of the yard and down the road. Through the rearview mirror I saw him shaking his fist at me and cursing. I got to the highway, and swung the car toward the bridge back to Los Angeles.

Chapter Twenty-one

Like a homing bird I flew to Bunker Hill, to my old hotel, to the kindest woman I had ever known. I parked the car in front of the hotel, pulled out two suitcases, and carried them inside. The lobby was vacant. I stood there a moment, breathing the fragrance of the place, the tender reminiscent scent of Helen Brownell's incense. I looked around lovingly. What solidarity. What permanence. It was as if that lobby would last forever, as if always waiting for me. I crossed to the desk, set down my suitcases, and rang the bell. The door behind the desk opened cautiously and I saw her peering at me uncertainly, as if not quite seeing.

"Hello, Helen," I smiled.

She kept looking at me. Then she closed the door. I waited a moment. When she did not reappear I rang the bell again. The door opened. She looked at me sternly. I noticed her hair. It was pure white now, white as lamb's wool.

"Helen," I said, and moved around to her side of the desk. "Oh, Helen, I'm so glad to see you again." I put my hands on her shoulders and bent to kiss her.

"Don't," she said. "Please don't."

"I love you."

She turned her back to me. "Go away," she implored. "I don't want you here. I can't do it any more."

"Please let me stay. Let me have my old room back."

"Impossible. It's rented. Please leave."

"Let's talk awhile," I coaxed. "Make me a cup of coffee, please."

"Why are you so stubborn? Can't you see that I don't

want you here?" She spun around and hurried to the door behind the desk. "Go away, Arturo. Find somebody your own age. I'm not for you. I never was." She closed the door.

It hurt very much. I sat down on a divan and tried to think it out. How could I entice her back? What could I say to her? Suddenly I was very tired. What had I done to her? Why couldn't we carry on as usual? We had had a little tiff, that was all. Why couldn't we be friends, just talking to one another, sitting on the veranda in the evening, watching the city light up below, and talking like old friends? Why was she cutting me off? I didn't care that she was so much older. I would love her forever. When she was ninety I would still love her, like the woman in Yeats's poem:

> When you are old and grey and full of sleep,
> And nodding by the fire, take down this book,
> And slowly read, and dream of the soft look
> Your eyes had once, and of their shadows deep;
>
> How many loved your moments of glad grace,
> And loved your beauty with love false or true,
> But one man loved the pilgrim soul in you,
> And loved the sorrows of your changing face.

Chapter Twenty-two

I found a room on Temple Street, above a Filipino restaurant. It was two dollars a week without towels, sheets, or pillow cases. I took it, sat on the bed and brooded about my life on the earth. Why was I here? What now? Who did I know? Not even myself. I looked at my hands. They were soft writer's hands, the hands of a writer peasant, not suited for hard work, not equal to making phrases. What could I do? I looked around the room, the wine-stained walls, the carpetless floor, the little window looking out on Figueroa Street. I smelled the cooking from the Filipino restaurant below. Was this the end of Arturo Bandini? Would this be the place where I was to die, on this gray mattress? I could lie here for weeks before anyone discovered me. I got to my knees and prayed:

"What have I done to you, Lord? Why do you punish me? All I ask is the chance to write, to have a friend or two, to cease my running. Bring me peace, oh Lord. Shape me into something worthwhile. Make the typewriter sing. Find the song within me. Be good to me, for I am lonely."

It seemed to hearten me. I went to the typewriter and sat before it. A gray wall loomed up. I pushed back my chair and walked down into the street. I got into my car and drove around.

I had trouble sleeping in the little room, even though I bought sheets and blankets. The trouble was, the misery of the day, the fruitlessness of working remained in the room during the night. In the morning it was still there, and I went to the street again. Then I remembered one of Ed-gington's axioms: "When stuck, hit the road." At sunset I wheeled my car out of the parking lot and hit the streets. Hour after hour I drove around. The city was like a tremendous park, from the foothills ot the sea, beautiful in the night, the lamps glowing like white balloons, the streets wide and plentiful and moving off in all directions. It did not matter which way you went, the road always stretched ahead, and you found yourself in strange little towns and neighborhoods, and it was soothing and refreshing, but it did not bring story ideas. Moving with the traffic, I wondered how many like myself took to the road merely to escape the city. Day and night the city teemed with traffic and it was impossible to believe that all those people had any rhyme or reason for driving.

In February Liberty Films released Velda van der Zee's picture, *Sin City*. I caught it at the Wiltern, on Wilshire, the early evening show. I went prepared to loathe it, and I was pleased to find the theater less than half full. I bought a sack of popcorn and found a seat in the loges. I sat there pleased that my name had been scrubbed from the film, and as the lights darkened, I felt very pleased and relieved that my name would not be among the credits. I laughed loudly when Velda's name appeared, and as the picture unreeled and the stagecoach bounded over the terrain, I laughed again loudly. A hand touched my shoulder. I turned to see a woman frowning.

"You're disturbing me," she said.

"I can't help it," I answered. "It's a very funny picture."

Now the hostile band of Indians appeared, and I guffawed. Several people in the vicinity got up and scattered to different seats.

And so it went. All of my work, all of my thinking, was so remote from the picture, that it was stunning, unbelievable. In only two places did I come upon lines that I might possibly have written, that the director did not delete. The first was in an early scene when the sheriff rode into Sin City at full gallop and brought his horse to a halt at the saloon, shouting "Whoa!" Now I remembered that line: "Whoa!" My line. A little further on the sheriff stalked out of the saloon, mounted his horse, and shouted "Giddyup!" That was my line too: "Giddyup." Whoa and giddyup—my fulfillment as a screenwriter.

It was not a good picture, or an exciting picture, or a mature picture, and as it came to an end and the house lights went on, I saw the weary patrons half asleep in their seats, showing no pleasure at all. I was glad. It proved my integrity. I was a better man for having refused the credit, a better writer. Time would prove it. When Velda van der Zee was a forgotten name in tinsel town, the world would still reckon with Arturo Bandini. I walked out into the night, and God, I felt good and refreshed and restored! Whoa and giddyup! Here we go again. I got into my car and took off in the traffic along Wilshire Boulevard, hell bent for my hotel.

I went up to my room and fell on the bed exhausted. I had been deluding myself. There was no pleasure in seeing *Sin City*. I was really not pleased at Velda's failure. In truth I felt sorry for her, for all writers, for the misery of the craft. I lay in that tiny room and it engulfed me like a tomb.

I got up and went down into the street. Half a block away was a Filipino saloon. I sat at the bar and ordered a glass of Filipino wine. The Filipinos around me laughed and played the dart game. I drank more wine. It was sweet and tinged with peppermint, warm in the stomach, tingling. I drank five more glasses, and stood up to leave. I felt nausea, and my stomach seemed to float into my chest. I got out on the sidewalk, leaned against the lamppost and felt the strength ooze from my knees.

Then everything vanished, and I was in a bed somewhere. It was a white room with big windows and it was daylight. There were tubes in my nose and down my throat and I felt the pain of vomiting. A nurse stood at the bedside and watched me gag and writhe until there was no more of it, only the terrible pain in my stomach and throat. The nurse removed the tubes.

"Where am I" I asked.

"Georgia Street Hospital," she said.

"What's the matter with me?"

"Poison," she said. "Your friend is here."

I looked toward the door. There stood Helen Brownell. She came quietly to the bedside and sat down. I took her hand and began to sob.

"There now," she soothed. "Everything's all right."

"What's the matter with me?" I choked. "What's going on?"

"Don't you remember?"

"I drank some wine—that's all."

"You drank too much," she said. "You passed out, and the wine made you very ill."

"Who brought me here?"

"The police ambulance."

"How did you find out?"

"My address was in your wallet."

"How long have you been here?"

"Since midnight," she said.

"Can I leave now?"

The nurse stepped up. "Not for a while," she said. "The doctor has to look at you first."

Mrs. Brownell stood up and squeezed my hand. "I must go now."

"I'll see you at the hotel."

She bit her lip. "Perhaps you shouldn't."

"Why not? I love you."

"Don't say that," she answered.

"It's true," I insisted. "I love you more than anybody in the world. I always have. I always will."

Without answering, she turned with a wisp of a smile, and walked out of the room. I felt my stomach heaving, and the nurse held my head as I vomited into a basin.

It was late afternoon when the doctor checked me out and permitted me to leave. When I asked about the charges for my stay he answered that they had been paid.

"By whom?" I said.

"Mrs. Brownell."

I got dressed and walked down the hall to the front door, where I took a trolley to Hill Street. At Third I got off and rode the cablecar to the top of Bunker Hill.

Chapter Twenty-three

A man stood behind the desk in the hotel lobby. He was thin and tall with a halo of gray hair. I asked to see Mrs. Brownell.

"She ain't here," he said.

"When are you expecting her?"

"Can't say. She went to San Francisco."

There was something familiar about him. "Are you a relative?" I asked.

"I'm her brother," he said. "Is your name Bandini?"

"That's right."

He lifted the desk blotter, and removed an envelope and handed it to me. My name was on it. I tore open the envelope. Inside was a statement from the Georgia Street Hospital, marked paid, a bill for twelve dollars. I looked inside the envelope for an explanation. There was none. The man watched me.

"Did she leave any message beside this?"

"That's all."

I took out my wallet and paid him the twelve dollars. Without thanking me he put it into the cash drawer. I nodded at the door to Mrs. Brownell's apartment, and stared sternly.

"Are you sure she's not in there?"

He pushed the door open and folded his arms. "See for yourself."

I shook my head. "It's not like her to do a thing like this."

The old man smiled. "That's what you think, sonny."

I walked out into the street. The sun was tumbling into

the ocean thirty miles west, and the city was in a tumult of radiant sunset colors, shards of clouds gathering on the far horizon, a touch of rain in the air. From beneath Bunker Hill I heard the uproar of the city, the clanging of trolley bells, the roar of cars, the lower depths. Beneath my feet was the Third Street tunnel, the sudden hush of traffic entering, and the roar of traffic emerging.

What am I doing here, I asked. I hate this place, this friendless city. Why was it always thrusting me away like an unwanted orphan? Had I not paid my dues? Had I not worked hard, tried hard? What did it have against me? Was it the incessant sense of my peasantry, the old conviction that somehow I did not belong?

If not Los Angeles, then what? Where could I find welcome, where could I sit among people who loved me and cared for me and took pride in me? Then it came to me. There *was* a place, and there were people who loved me, and I would go to them. So fuck you, Los Angeles, fuck your palm trees, and your highassed women, and your fancy streets, for I am going home, back to Colorado, back to the best damned town in the USA—Boulder, Colorado.

Chapter Twenty-four

I put my car in storage and got aboard a Greyhound bus with two suitcases. The bus pulled out of Los Angeles at seven in the evening of a very hot day. In fact, it was the last hot day I would experience for a month. The interior of the bus was even hotter than the day, the leather seats heaving with heat when one sat down, and the passengers sprawled in exhaustion and discomfort by the time we reached the city limits. They looked as if they had been aboard for days, billows of cigarette smoke filling the air.

When we crossed into Nevada, the first snowflakes began to fall. Through Nevada we drove in the gathering storm, the snow piling up, the bus slowing down in a blinding storm. When we reached Utah and made a stop the snow was above the wheels. We rushed into the depot, drank cups of revolting coffee, and got aboard again. The hours passed, the snow fell with insidious determination, as if to bury us on the plain. In Wyoming snowplows came out of Rock Springs to rescue us, and the journey was slowed to a crawl. By the time we pulled in at the Boulder depot I had to struggle to my feet as I staggered out.

The snow was terrifying, the flakes as big as dollars, wafting slowly toward earth, and lying there, not melting. I stood in front of the bus depot shivering in a light sweater, blinking at my home town. Where the hell was it? The snow played tricks with the scene. I knew there was a bridge half a block away, but now it was invisible. I knew there was a lumberyard across the street, but it had vanished. I shivered, and lit a cigarette, and pounded my feet to keep them warm. Suddenly a figure stood before me. I thought I knew his face, but I wasn't sure until he said:

"What are you doing here?"

That could only be my father.

"I've come home."

His breath burst like steam.

"You're cold," he said. "Where's your overcoat?"

"You're wearing it," I said. He unbuttoned the heavy sheepskin coat, and peeled it off.

"Put it on," he said, holding it out for me.

"What about you?"

"Never mind me. Put it on."

He helped me get into it. He was in shirtsleeves now, the snowflakes banging him.

"Let's go," he said. We quickly walked away. The overcoat felt warm from the heat of his body. It was all of a piece, a part of my life, like an old chair, or a worn fork, or my mother's shawl, the things of my life, the precious worthless treasured things.

"What'd you come home for?"

"I wanted to. I had to. I got lonesome."

"You leave your job in the pitchers?"

"For a while—until later, maybe."

"There's nothing for you here," my father said, his breath steaming. "What are you going to do now?"

"I'll think of something," I said.

"You won't listen to me," he half groaned. "You never did listen to your father."

"I had to do it my own way."

He cursed. "And what's it got you?"

The storm heaved and sighed. I looked at Arapahoe Street. The big elms seemed so much bigger in the snow light. The houses huddled like animals in the storm. A car clattered by, its chains clanging. A mile away were the first tall hills of the Rocky Mountains, but the snow hid them away in a white veil. Across the street in the Delaney yard stood old Elsie, their cow, patiently in the storm, watching us pass by.

What a wonderful street! How much of my life I had spent here, under the quiet elms, our house a block away—Christmases and baseball and first communion and Hallowe'en, and kites and sleigh rides, and ballgames and Easter and graduation and all of my life evoked by this wondrous street of old houses, with dim lights in windows, and home at the end of the block.

We reached the house, and there it was, parked in the street, my brother's decrepit Overland touring car, the top down, the inside overflowing with new snow. No matter. It had a life of its own. Once the snow melted, it would start up and merrily chug away. My father and I mounted the porch steps and pounded the snow from our shoes before entering. Opening the door, my father shouted:

"Here he is!"

In the kitchen I saw my mother at the stove, a ladling spoon in her hand. She turned and saw me. With a cry to God, she flung out her arms and sent the ladling spoon flying, and came running toward me.

"I knew it," she said. "I've been saying it all day."

We met and embraced in the dining room, hugging and kissing, as she sobbed and her tears splashed my face. My brother Mario stood aside, embarrassed. He had grown a great deal since I last saw him, a bashful, inarticulate kid of nineteen. My sister Stella slipped into my arms. She was sixteen, very beautiful and very shy, but not ashamed of her tears. Over her shoulder I saw my little brother Tom, a seventh grader at Sacred Heart School. We embraced, and he said:

"You're littler than I thought."

My mother took me by the hand and led me into the kitchen.

"You think I didn't know?" she said. "You think I'd go to all this trouble if I didn't know you were coming?" She gestured at the cast iron baking dish on the stove. "Look!"

It was lasagne, red tomato sauce bubbling in an ocean of pasta.

"How could you know I was coming?" I asked. "I didn't

know myself until the last minute."

"I prayed. How else?"

My brother Tom took my hand and pulled me into the dining room, and through to the bedroom. In a whisper he asked, "Did you ever see Hedy Lamarr?"

"All the time," I said.

"You're a liar." Then, "What's she like?"

"Unbelievable. When she walks into a room the whole building shakes."

"I wrote her a letter. She didn't even answer it."

"Before I leave you write her again. I'll take it to her house."

He grinned, and then, "You're a liar."

I put my hand over my heart. "I swear to God."

We were poor, but as always we ate very well, the table overflowing with salad and homemade bread and lasagne, and my father's dandelion wine. When we were finished it was time to talk, to question the prodigal son. They did not regard me as a failure. I was a hero, a conqueror back from distant battlefields. They even gave me a sense of my importance in the world.

"Now then," my father said, finishing his wine, "what'd you come home for?"

"To see my family, got any objections?"

He looked right at me. "Got any money?"

"Some."

"We need it. Give it to your mother."

I pulled out my wallet and removed two one-hundred-dollar bills, and pushed them toward my mother. She began to cry.

"It's too much," she said.

My father flared. "Shut up and take it."

My mother pushed the bills into her apron pocket.

"Arturo," Stella said, "do you know Clark Gable?"

"Very well—a good friend of mine."

"Is he really that nice? Is he stuck up?"

"He's as shy as a bird."

My father filled his glass again. "How about Tom Mix?

You ever see him?"

"At the studio every day. Him and Tony."

My father smiled, remembering. "Tony. Great horse."

My brother Tom looked sheepish and asked, "How tall is Hedy Lamarr?"

"A lot taller than you."

"Smart ass," Tom said.

My father whacked the table. "Don't use that kind of language in this house." There was a respectful silence. Then Mario spoke:

"You ever run into James Cagney?"

"Frequently."

"What kind of a car does he drive?"

"Duesenberg."

"Figures," Mario said.

Chapter Twenty-five

Home was a good place. I slept well. I ate well. The first few days I lounged about the house, showing off my wardrobe. The stuff in my bulging suitcases fascinated my mother— my suits, my sportscoats, my slacks. She sewed buttons and darned socks, pressed and cleaned my suits, and hung them up. With every change of wardrobe my mother was awed. She touched the fabrics, she gloated over me. I was two characters. When I wore corduroys and a T-shirt I was her boy, but when I put on my splendidly draped suits I was a prince.

"God has been good to me," she would sigh. "You look so important."

As time passed I tired of loafing about the house, and began to spend my days in town, visiting old haunts: Benny's poolhall on Pearl Street, the bowling alley on Walnut. I went to the library and found again the books that had changed my life: Sherwood Anderson, Jack London, Knut Hamsun, Dostoevsky, D'Annunzio, Pirandello, Flaubert, de Maupassant. The welcome they gave me was much warmer than the cold curiosity of old friends I met in the town.

One day I ran into Joe Kelly, the reporter for the *Boulder Times*. We shook hands and were glad to see one another. In high school Kelly and I used to hitchhike to Denver to watch Western League baseball. Joe took me to the office of the *Times*, had my picture taken, and interviewed me. It was not a flattering interview, nor was it unkind, but there was a challenging quality to it, as if many questions about myself and my work needed more answers. My father bought twenty-five copies of the interview when it appeared, and everyone in the family sat at the dining-room table reading his copy.

The next day Agnes Lawson telephoned. We were old members of the Red Pencil, a literary society sponsored by the church. I had not seen her in two years. She was a haughty, spoiled girl with wealthy parents, and when she invited me to a party at her house, my first impulse was to refuse. The same nasal twang was in her voice, the same snobbish reserve.

"A lot of Red Pencil alumni are coming," she said. "We want to see you now that you're famous."

"I'll try to make it," I said. "I'm supposed to go to another party, but I can drop in at your place for a while."

The invitation thrilled my mother, for Agnes was the daughter of one of Boulder's leading citizens, as well as owner of its best known clothing store.

The next night I dressed carefully for Agnes's party. Gray tweed suit, red necktie, gray shirt. My mother beamed.

"What an honor!" she said. "Isn't it nice, going into those lovely houses! I'm so proud of you."

My brother Mario swept the snow from his Overland, covered the front seat with a tarp, and drove me to the three-story Lawson house on University Hill. I looked at that house with unpleasant memories, a house that had been forbidden before. I remembered many summers when Agnes threw parties that always excluded me, nor could I forget the large clothing bill my family owed the Lawson store. Mr. Lawson never spoke of the bill, but he always managed a look of annoyance whenever he saw me.

I rang the doorbell, and Agnes answered. Standing beside her, his arm around her waist, was Biff Newhouse, a star fullback on the Colorado University football team. Biff sported a letterman's sweater, with a gold "C" across his chest. Agnes held out her hand and said "Hi."

"Hello, Agnes."

She was a small girl, with bobbed hair, fashionably dressed in a black frock.

"This is Biff Newhouse."

Biff and I shook hands. His grip was unnecessarily harsh.

"What do you say?" he grinned.

"Hello, Biff," I said.

There were a dozen people gathered in the living room. I had known all of them through grade school and high school. They looked at me without expression, as if to deny me even the slightest hint of warmth or reunion. Only Joe Kelly stepped up and shook my hand.

"I liked what you wrote about me," I said.

"Good. I was afraid you wouldn't."

"What about a drink?" Agnes said.

"Fine. I'll have a Scotch and soda."

She moved to the bar and mixed the drink. A tall girl wearing glasses walked up.

"I hear you're a screenwriter," she said.

"Best in Hollywood."

She smiled faintly. "I knew you'd say something like that. Are you still writing that miserable poetry?"

"What's miserable about it? I sold one to the *New Yorker.*"

Agnes brought my drink. I gulped it down quickly. We sat on divans and big chairs in front of the fireplace. Agnes mixed another drink for me.

"How are things in tinsel town?" she asked.

"Fabulous," I said. "You should come out some time."

She laughed. "Me in Hollywood? That's funny."

"What kinda money you screenwriters make?" Biff asked.

"I started modestly," I said. "Three hundred a week. My current salary is a thousand a week."

Biff smiled doubtfully. "Bullshit," he said.

"Maybe bullshit to you, but it's good money to me."

"Do you know Joel McCrea?" the tall poetess asked.

"I not only know him, he happens to be one of my best friends."

Agnes gave me another drink, and I sipped it.

"How about Ginger Rogers?" Agnes coaxed. "Tell us about Ginger Rogers, Arturo."

I looked into her mocking eyes.

"Ginger Rogers is a superior person. She has charm and beauty and talent. I regard her as one of the great artists of our time. However, my favorite star is Norma Shearer. Her beauty is breathtaking. Her eyes are marvellous, and she has a figure that's ravishing. I know lots of actresses with ravishing figures—Bette Davis, Hedy Lamarr, Claudette Colbert, Jean Harlow, Katharine Hepburn, Carole Lombard, Maureen O'Sullivan, Myrna Loy, Janet Gaynor, Alice Faye, Irene Dunne, Mary Astor, Gloria Swanson, Margaret Lindsay, Dolores del Rio. I know them all. They're part of my life. I've dined with them, danced with them, made love with them, and I'll tell you this—I never disappointed any of them. You go among them, ask them questions about Arturo Bandini, ask them if they were ever turned away in disappointment."

I paused and drained off another Scotch highball. Then I stood up.

"What's the matter with you people?" I crossed to the bar and leaned against it. "How can you live such dull lives? Is there no romance? Is there no beauty among you?" I looked straight at Biff Newhouse. "Can't you think of anything else but football? Not me, buster. I live a different life. And without your fucking snow. I play in the sun. I play golf with Bing Crosby and Warner Baxter and Edmund Lowe. I play tennis with Nils Asther and George Brent and William Powell and Pat O'Brien and Paul Muni. I play by day, I fuck in the twilight, and I work by night. I swim with Johnny Weismuller and Esther Williams and Buster Crabbe. Everybody loves me. Understand? Everybody."

I swung around in a grand gesture, and my heels slipped out from under me, and I sat on the floor, my glass splattering. I heard their laughter, and tried to get to my feet, but I slipped again and fell. Biff Newhouse lifted me to a standing position. Suddenly I loathed him, and swung at him, and hit him in the jaw. His eyes boiled in fury and he let me have it—one short punch, squarely in the nose, and I was down on the floor again, blood coursing from my nose, down my chest, on to my pants, the sleeve of my coat. In a daze I saw the others swirling, walking around me, walking out of the house. Then Joe Kelly hoisted me to my feet, pushed a bar towel under my nose and steadied me as I wiped the blood away.

"I'll take you home," he said. He held me up as we walked outside and down the porch steps. Cars were starting up and leaving. Joe helped me to his Ford. The blood was still pouring. I pressed the towel into my nose as we drove away.

We got to my house and I stepped out, careful not to slam the car door. Kelly drove off and I stopped to gather snow in my two hands and press it against my nose until the bleeding stopped. Quietly I walked through the snow to my brother's window and tapped on the glass. He came to the side door. Choking in alarm, he looked at my bloody face.

"What happened?" he said.

"I fell down and cracked my nose. Be quiet. I don't want Mama to hear. Is the old man home?"

"He's in bed."

"I'm leaving here," I whispered. "I'm getting out—tonight, right now. Be quiet."

We entered the side door. I opened my suitcases on the bed and quietly transferred my clothes from the dresser and closet to the luggage. Mario dressed and watched me wash the blood from my face and hands. I changed clothes, and bundled my bloodstained suit and shirt and put them in the suitcase.

"Let's go," I whispered. He hefted one suitcase and I took the other. Without a sound we stepped out into the snow, and walked to his old car. Mario's voice trembled.

"What'll I tell Mama?" he asked.

"Nothing," I said.

"Are you sure you fell down?" he asked. "Are you sure somebody didn't pop you?"

"Absolutely."

We threw the luggage into the car and drove to the bus depot. The Denver bus was parked in front, panting like an animal. I bought a ticket to Los Angeles and climbed aboard. Mario stood beneath my window, looking up at me with tears in his eyes. I rushed out of the bus and stepped down and threw my arms around him.

"Thanks, Mario. I won't forget this."

He sobbed and put his head on my shoulder. "Be careful," he said. "Don't fight, Arturo."

"I can take care of myself."

I turned and got aboard the bus. That was Wednesday night. We drove through snow most of the way and arrived in Los Angeles on a sunburst Saturday morning.

Chapter Twenty-six

So I was back again, back to LA, with two suitcases and seventeen dollars. I liked it, the sweep of blue skies, the sun in my face, the endearing streets, tempting, beckoning, the concrete and cobblestones, soft and comforting as old shoes. I picked up my grips and walked along Fifth Street. Purposefully I walked, wondering why I could almost never bring myself to call her Helen. I had to break the habit. I would walk to the top of Bunker Hill and open my arms to her and say, "Helen, I love you."

We would start over again. Maybe we'd buy a little house in Woodland Hills, the Kansas type, with a chickenyard and a dog. Oh, Helen, I've missed you so, and now I know what I want. Maybe she wouldn't like Woodland Hills. Maybe she preferred the hotel. It had aged so well, like an aristocrat, like Helen herself. I would choose a room for writing and we would complete our days together. Oh, Helen. Forgive me for ever leaving you. It will never happen again.

I rode on the trolley to the crest of Bunker Hill, and looked at the hotel in the distance. It was magic, like a castle in a book of fairy tales. I knew she would have me this time. I felt the strength of my years, and I knew I was stronger than she, and that she would melt in my arms. I entered the hotel and lowered my suitcases against the wall. She was not behind the desk. I had to smile as I crossed to the desk and rang the bell. When there was no answer I struck the bell again, harder. The door opened slightly. There stood the man I had seen before, the man who said he was her brother. He did not come forward, and spoke in a whisper.

"Yes?"

"I'm looking for Helen."

"She's not here," he said, and closed the door. I walked around the desk and knocked. He opened the door and stood there crying.

"She's gone. She's dead."

"How?" I said. "When?"

"A week ago. She died of a stroke."

I felt myself weakening, as I staggered toward an armchair at the window. I didn't want to cry. Something deep and abiding had caved in, swallowing me up. I felt my chest heaving. The brother came over and stood beside me, crying.

"I'm sorry," he said.

I got up, hefted my suitcase, and walked out. At the little depot on Angel's Flight I saw on a park bench and let my grief have its way. For two hours I was there, griefstricken and bewildered. I had thought of many things since knowing her, but never her death. For all her years, she nourished a love in me. Now it was gone. Now that she was dead I could think of her no longer. I had sobbed and whimpered and wept until it was all gone, all of it, and as always I found myself alone in the world.

The manager of the Filipino hotel was glad to see me. It was no surprise when he said that my room was unoccupied. It was my kind of room. I deserved it—the smallest, most uninviting room in Los Angeles. I started up the stairs and pushed opend the door to the dreadful hole.

"You forgot something," the manager said. He stood in the doorway holding my portable typewriter. It startled me, not because it was there, but because I had completely forgotten it. He placed it on the table and I thanked him. Closing the door, I opened a suitcase and took out a copy of Knut Hamsun's *Hunger*. It was a treasured piece, constantly with me since the day I stole it from the Boulder library. I had read it so many times that I could recite it. But it did not matter now. Nothing mattered.

I stretched out on the bed and slept. It was twilight when I awakened and turned on the light. I felt better, no longer tired. I went to the typewriter and sat before it. My thought was to write a sentence, a single perfect sentence. If I could write one good sentence I could write two and if I could write two I could write three, and if I could write three I could write forever. But suppose I failed? Suppose I had lost all of my beautiful talent? Suppose it had burned up in the fire of Biff Newhouse smashing my nose or Helen Brownell dead forever? What would happen to me? Would I go to Abe Marx and become a busboy again? I had seventeen dollars in my wallet. Seventeen dollars and the fear of writing. I sat erect before the typewriter and blew on my fingers. Please God, please Knut Hamsun, don't desert me now. I started to write and I wrote:

> "The time has come," the Walrus said,
>   "To talk of many things:
> Of shoes—and ships—and sealing wax—
>   Of cabbages—and kings—"

I looked at it and wet my lips. It wasn't mine, but what the hell, a man had to start someplace.

Printed December 1981 in Santa Barbara &
Ann Arbor for the Black Sparrow Press by
Graham Mackintosh & Edwards Brothers Inc.
Design by Barbara Martin. This edition is
published in paper wrappers; there are 500
cloth trade copies; 200 hardcover copies have
been numbered & signed by the author; & 26
lettered copies have been handbound in boards
by Earle Gray & are signed by John Fante.

John Fante: ca. 1942

John Fante was born in Colorado in 1909. He attended parochial school in Boulder, and Regis High School, a Jesuit boarding school. He also attended the University of Colorado for a time and Long Beach City College.

Fante began writing in 1929 and published his first short story in *The American Mercury* in 1932. He had no difficulty in getting into print and published numerous short stories in *The Atlantic Monthly, The American Mercury, The Saturday Evening Post, Colliers, Esquire,* and *Harper's Bazaar.* His first novel, *Wait Until Spring, Bandini,* was published in 1938. The following year *Ask the Dust* appeared (and was reprinted 40 years later in 1980 by Black Sparrow Press). In 1940 a collection of his short stories, *Dago Red,* was brought out by Viking Press. *Full of Life* appeared in 1952, and *The Brotherhood of the Grape* in 1977.

Meanwhile Fante has been occupied extensively in screenwriting. Some of his credits include *Full of Life, Jeanne Eagels, My Man and I, The Reluctant Saint, Something for a Lonely Man, My Six Loves,* and *Walk on the Wild Side.*

He is married and the father of a daughter and three sons, and has lived in Malibu, California for over thirty years. He was stricken with diabetes in 1955 and its complications brought about blindness in 1978, but he continues to write by dictation to his wife, Joyce. He is presently at work on a new novel.